D0745417

*O HUMAN STAR

VOLUME ONE

NO LONGER PROPERTY OF
SEATTLE PUBLIC LIBRARY

Story and artwork by Blue Delliquanti

Printed in China on responsibly sourced paper
First edition: March 2015

ISBN: 978-0-9909956-0-9

© 2015 Blue Delliquanti. All rights reserved. No portion of this book may be reproduced by any means without written permission from the author, except in the case of short excerpts as part of a review. The events, characters and institutions presented in this book are fictional. Any resemblance to actual persons - living, dead, or resurrected - is purely coincidental.

"In the Morning of the Magicians"
Words and music by Wayne Coyne and Steven Drozd
© 2002 EMI BLACKWOOD MUSIC INC. and LOVELY SORTS OF DEATH MUSIC
All rights controlled and administered by EMI BLACKWOOD MUSIC INC.
All rights reserved. International copyright secured. Used by permission.
Reprinted by permission of Hal Leonard Corporation

This book collects Chapters 1 through 3 of O Human Star, which first appeared online from January 2012 to February 2014 at ohumanstar.com

Thanks to
Taneka Stotts, Rhiannon Rasmussen-Silverstein,
Christianne Goudreau, Christina McKenzie,
C. Spike Trotman, Matt Sheridan, and Mary Holland,
who helped this book be its best.

Thanks to
the Brush Creek Foundation for the Arts
and the Prism Comics Queer Press Grant,
whose existence helped sustain the comic
during its earliest days.

And special thanks to
my friends, my readers, and my family,
who loved me when I was far away.

CHAPTER ONE
His Own Image

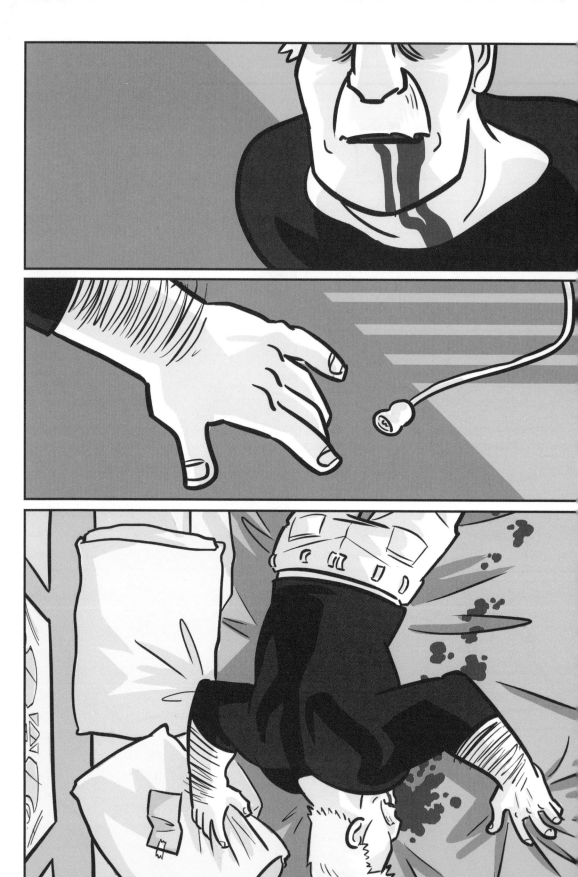

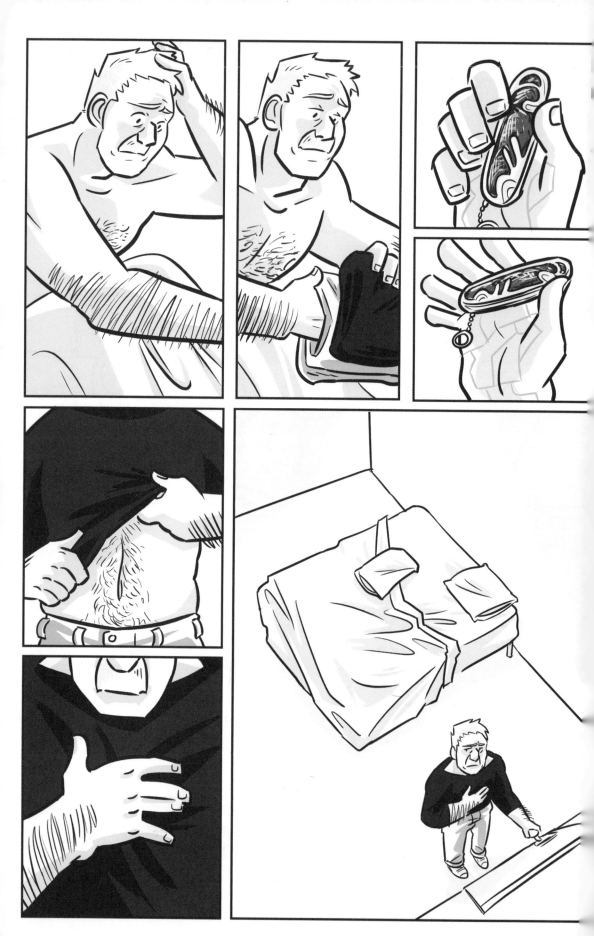

GOOD MORNING, ALASTAIR STERLING.

LET US APOLOGIZE FOR THE INCONVENIENCE. BY NECESSITY OUR MANUFACTURING CENTERS MUST BE LOCATED FAR FROM OUR HEADQUARTERS IN THE CITY.

PLEASE ALLOW US TO ESCORT YOU HOME.

YOU KNOW –

WHEN I WAS NINE I DESIGNED A ROBOT THAT LOOKED LIKE THAT. IT WAS ONE OF MY FIRST PROTOTYPES.

COURSE, IT NEVER ENDED UP LOOKING QUITE LIKE *THAT*. THE ONE THAT'S... DRIVING THE CAR RIGHT NOW.

THE FUTURISTIC HOVERCAR.

AND *YOU* –

I SEE.

THE BODY YOU WOKE UP IN THIS MORNING IS A SYNTHETIC REPLICA OF YOUR ORIGINAL BODY.

THIS INCLUDES A DIGITAL COPY OF YOUR MEMORIES AND MIND THAT WAS PRIVATELY ARCHIVED AFTER YOU –

TOOK ILL.

OUR MANUFACTURING CENTER SIMULATED THE SPACIAL CONDITIONS OF YOUR LAST MEMORIES SO THAT YOUR DISORIENTATION UPON ACTIVATION WOULD BE MINIMAL.

AND EVERY *PHYSICAL* FEATURE OF YOUR BODY HAS BEEN RECREATED IN METICULOUS DETAIL.

EVERYTHING SHOULD FEEL REASSURINGLY FAMILIAR.

MY PAPERS. MY MACHINES, ALL OF MY **WORK** —

—ARE IN THE RIGHT HANDS, AS YOU HAD STIPULATED IN YOUR WILL.

YOU WILL FIND, UPON ENTERING THE CITY AGAIN, THAT MUCH HAS **CHANGED** DURING YOUR ABSENCE.

SYNTHETIC BEINGS — ROBOTS, YOU CALLED THEM — HAVE ADVANCED TO A LEVEL OF INTELLI-GENCE AND AUTONOMY UNIMAGINABLE IN YOUR LIFETIME.

MOST OF YOUR OWN WORK — YOUR DESIGNS, YOUR IDEAS — HAS BEEN THE FOUNDATION FOR THE LAST TWO GENERATIONS OF ROBOTS.

YOUR LEGACY, AS CONTINUED BY MR. PINSKY.

BREN-DAN?

IT WAS MR. PINSKY'S ESTATE THAT COMMISSIONED US TO RECONSTRUCT YOU IN THE FIRST PLACE.

BEST IN SHOW

TO FILL A VOID IN THE ROBOTICS COMMUNITY THAT WAS LEFT BEHIND AFTER YOUR DEATH.

TO ENSURE THAT YOUR GENIUS WAS NOT LOST.

TAKE ME TO HIM.

MR. STERLING, WHERE DID YOU *THINK* WE HAD BEEN TAKING YOU?

I PRESUME THAT WE ARE NO LONGER NEEDED HERE.

NO.

THANKS.

MR. STERLING...

WE ARE ALL HAPPY TO HAVE YOU BACK.

ALL OF US.

KLANK

KANK

KANK

KANK

KLUNK

TEN
SECONDS.

ARE YOU
JUST GOING
TO STAND
THERE?

GIMEL, ALLOW CLEARANCE FOR OUR GUEST. HE'S COMING IN WITH ME.

FOR LUNCH, MR. PINSKY?

WHAT?

IT IS NEARLY TWO O'CLOCK AND YOU HAVE YET TO TAKE ANY –

FINE, FINE, FINE. SET IT AT THE TABLE. AND SEND SULLA ON AN ERRAND, PLEASE.

YES, SIR.

EXCUSE ME, SIR.

THAT'S YOUR GIMEL? IT LOOKS LIKE OUR OLD GIMEL 75. FROM THE WORKSHOP.

A FEW GENERATIONS LATER AND YOU'VE MADE HIM INTO A BUTLER.

HOW – HOW DO YOU KNOW ALL THESE THINGS? TELL ME THE TRUTH.

HOW DID YOU KNOW TO SAY... WHAT YOU SAID OUT THERE?

BRENDAN, IT'S ME. I KNOW THAT – I KNOW THAT I'M DEAD.

BUT I'VE SEEN WHAT I LOOK LIKE AND IT ALL LOOKS THE SAME. I STILL REMEMBER EVERYTHING.

I FEEL THE SAME.

THE SAME AS BEFORE.

22

SO... SO THE LAST THING YOU REMEMBER IS –

YEAH.

WHAT'S THIS?

PROCESSED FRUCTOSE WAFERS, SIR.

IT IS DESIGNED TO BE EFFICIENTLY PROCESSED BY COMPLEX SYNTHETIC BEINGS INTO USABLE ENERGY. NO WASTE.

IS IT GOOD?

IT'S SUGAR, SIR.

GREAT.

MY FAV-ORITE.

WHO'S SULLA? YOUR DAUGHTER?

I – NO!

OH, NO. NOT QUITE MY DAUGHTER.

YOUR WIFE?

GOD, NO. IT'S –

IT'S A LONG STORY.

AL –

AL, WHAT ARE YOU *DOING* HERE?

THEY TOLD ME IT WAS *YOU.*

THE THINGS THAT WOKE ME UP THIS MORNING AND DROVE ME HERE! THE BLACK ROBOT... *DOG THING* ... AND THE GODDAMN *BALLERINA!*

WHAT? WHO'S *THEY?*

A DOG AND A – *WHAT?*

THEY TOLD ME YOU HAD HIRED THEM TO BRING ME BACK.

BUT HOW WOULD ANYONE – AL, I HAVE NO IDEA WHO YOU'RE TALKING ABOUT. I DON'T KNOW THEM.

BUT YOU *WERE* TRYING TO BRING ME BACK.

WELL, I – I WAS.

I DID.

BUT AL, IT *ISN'T YOU.*

I HAD MY OWN COPY OF YOUR MIND THAT I MADE BEFORE YOU DIED, BUT IT WAS –

GOD, THIS IS SO COMPLICATED.

IT WAS *IMPERFECT.*

SIR, SULLA HAS RETURNED FROM HER ERRAND.

NO. OH GOD, NOT *NOW.*

WHEN I TELL YOU IDIOTS TO SEND SOMEONE AWAY, I MEAN THEY SHOULD BE GONE FOR MORE THAN *TWENTY MINUTES!*

WHAT THE HELL IS WRONG WITH YOU?

WE'RE TERRIBLY SORRY THAT WE DISAPPOINTED YOU. SHOULD WE FILE AN ERROR REPORT, SIR?

NO, JUST —

GODDAMMIT, SHE'S SEEN US.

LET'S JUST GET THIS NIGHTMARE OVER WITH.

SULLA!

HONEY, COME DOWN HERE. I WANT YOU TO MEET SOMEBODY.

FFFSSH

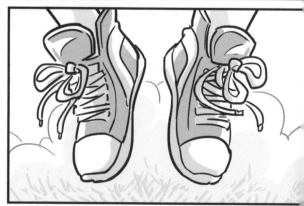

OH, WOW.

YOU LOOK JUST LIKE HIM. JUST LIKE –

SULLA, I'D LIKE YOU TO MEET AN UNEXPECTED GUEST. THIS IS MY OLD RESEARCH PARTNER, ALASTAIR STERLING.

FOR REAL?!

AL, THIS IS – THIS IS SULLA.

HAVE YOU BEEN WORKING ON HIM THIS WHOLE *TIME*?

WHY DIDN'T YOU ASK ME TO *HELP*, I WOULDA –

SULLA, NOW'S NOT A GOOD TIME.

ALASTAIR'S ONLY BEEN HERE A SHORT WHILE, AND I NEED TO DISCUSS SOME THINGS WITH HIM.

WHAT DID YOU GET WHILE YOU WERE DOWNTOWN?

SOME TULIPS AND BULBS AND STUFF FOR THE GARDEN.

WHY DON'T YOU GET GIMEL AND THE OTHERS TO HELP YOU PLANT THEM AND GET THE GARDEN SET UP?

OKAY!

INSIDE, AL, LET'S GO.

CHANGE YOUR CLOTHES FIRST!

SO.

AL, DON'T EVEN. THERE'S NO WAY TO EXPLAIN IT CONCISELY.

BUT THE ANSWER IS *YES*. SULLA IS — *WAS* — THE VERSION OF YOU I'D BEEN WORKING ON.

FOR THE LAST SIXTEEN YEARS.

SHE DOESN'T HAVE YOUR MEMORIES, BUT EVERYTHING ELSE IS THERE. SHE'S *YOU*.

SHE'S ONE OF THE MOST ADVANCED SYNTHETIC BEINGS IN THE WORLD NOW. AND IT'S ALL FROM YOUR WORK.

OUR WORK.

YOU **KNOW** THAT'S NOT THE ANSWER TO MY QUESTION.

AL . . .

WHY THE HELL IS THAT THING A **GIRL**, BRENDAN?

YOU CAN'T CALL THEM **THINGS**, AL, THEY HAVE RIGHTS UNDER STATE LAW NOW.

WHY IS IT A **GIRL**?

THREE YEARS AGO, SHE – SHE ASKED ME TO CHANGE HER. SO I DID. IT WAS **HER** CHOICE.

AFTER ALL THESE YEARS, I WONDERED –

I MEAN, SHE'S LIKE YOU IN EVERY **OTHER** WAY –

I'VE ALWAYS WONDERED IF **YOU** WERE –

DID I EVER GIVE THAT IMPRESSION TO YOU.

BRENDAN.

AL, COME ON –

THE WAY YOU WERE ABOUT EVERYTHING ELSE –

ABOUT ME –

I THOUGHT MAYBE –

THAT'S IT. I'M LEAVING. I'M DONE.

NOBODY KNOWS, ALASTAIR.

I JUST THOUGHT YOU'D BE HAPPY TO HEAR IT. ALL THESE YEARS, I'VE NEVER TOLD ANYONE.

IT'S JUST THE WAY YOU WANTED IT.

GOOD.

BRENDAN GAVE YOU CLEARANCE, YOU KNOW.

FFFFF

FFFFFLY.

YOU CAN FLY.

THAT'S RIGHT.

OKAY.

WHAT'RE YOU DOING OUT HERE?

LEAVING.

HUH? I THOUGHT YOU JUST GOT HERE!

HAS BRENDAN ALREADY SHOWN YOU AROUND THE HOUSE?

ARE YOU STAYING SOMEWHERE ELSE, WE CAN PUT YOU UP –

I DON'T NEED THAT.

I –

I DON'T BELONG HERE.

YOU DON'T MEAN THAT. HAVE YOU AT LEAST SEEN THE VIEW FROM THE BACKYARD?

NOT INTERESTED.

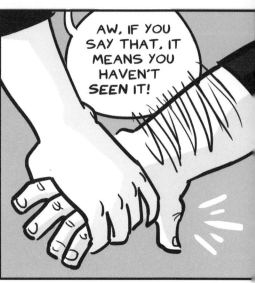

AW, IF YOU SAY THAT, IT MEANS YOU HAVEN'T SEEN IT!

THAT'S — THAT'S A *FIRM* GRIP —

COME ON, WE CAN TAKE THE SIDE PATH.

THAT WAY, WE DON'T HAVE TO GO BACK INSIDE.

I DON'T WANT TO GO BACK *ANYWHERE!*

I'VE SEEN THIS BIT.

BUT NOT THE BOTTOM BIT, RIGHT?

THAT'S THE BEST BIT!

I BET IT LOOKED REALLY DIFFERENT BACK THEN. HUH?

NO.

IT LOOKS THE SAME.

MORE OR LESS.

IT'S THE SAME.

SHE DEFINITELY *TALKS* MORE THAN I DO.

HA. WELL, THAT'S WHAT SHE GETS FOR BEING AROUND ME FOR ALMOST SIXTEEN YEARS.

LISTEN, IT'S BEEN A *VERY* LONG, *VERY* STRESSFUL DAY. FOR *ME*. I CAN'T EVEN IMAGINE WHAT IT MUST BE LIKE FOR *YOU* RIGHT NOW.

I'M GONNA FIGURE THIS OUT, BUT WE WON'T GET ANYTHING DONE TONIGHT. THIS BUILDING YOU WOKE UP IN - YOU HAVE NO IDEA WHERE IT WAS?

BY ONE OF THOSE ELEVATED HIGHWAY THINGS OUTSIDE OF TOWN. TO THE SOUTH. THAT'S ALL I GOT.

THEN YOU'RE STAYING HERE TONIGHT.

NO! I -

DON'T MAKE A FUSS. YOU DON'T HAVE ANYWHERE ELSE TO GO.

THE COUCH IS FINE. THANKS.

YEAH.

YEAH, NO PROBLEM.

YOU CAN SLEEP IN MY BED.

. . . WHILE I TAKE THE *COUCH*, I MEAN. *DOWNSTAIRS*. IN THE WORKSHOP. I'VE PULLED SOME ALL-NIGHTERS IN THERE BEFORE OH GOD...

FLIK

KSHIK

KCHAK

SHIK

CHIK

SSSHUK

"NOTHING IS STRANGER
TO MAN THAN
HIS OWN IMAGE."

- KAREL ČAPEK, *R.U.R.*
[ROSSUM'S UNIVERSAL ROBOTS]
1920

CHAPTER TWO
In the Morning of the Magicians

CHOP
CHOP
CHOP
CHOP
CHO
C

MR. STERLING?

WHOA, WHOA, HEY! IT'S OKAY!

IT'S JUST ME!

ALASTAIR?

YOU JUST NEED TO GET YOUR BEARINGS. YOU FELL ASLEEP.

YOU —

I FELL ASLEEP?

HOW?

YOU POWERED DOWN, LIKE THE REST OF US.

MOST OF THE MORE ADVANCED MODELS HAVE A SLEEP CYCLE TO LET THEIR DRIVES REGENERATE.

YOU WANNA EAT SOMETHING? BRENDAN TOLD ME YOU'D LIKE THIS FOR BREAKFAST.

49

HEY, YOU! DON'T TAKE HIS BREAK-FAST!

YOU'VE MADE SOME FRIENDS.

ARE YOU OKAY, MR. STERLING?

YEAH, YEAH.

I'M JUST NOT USED TO SEEING MYSELF AS A PREPUBESCENT GIRL.

NO FAIR! I'M NOT *PREPUBESCENT*.

WHATEVER. IT'S A LOT TO TAKE IN.

WHAT WITH BEING A... ROBOT ...NOW AND STILL NEEDING TO EAT AND SLEEP.

YEAH, YOU MUST HAVE CONKED OUT *REAL* GOOD. YOU DIDN'T EVEN CHANGE CLOTHES OR ANYTHING.

I DON'T HAVE ANY OTHER CLOTHES. THIS IS ALL THEY GAVE ME.

"THEY?"

THE GUYS WHO MADE ME.

AND THEY DIDN'T GIVE YOU ANYTHING BUT ONE SET OF CLOTHES?

HUH.

THAT SEEMS LIKE KIND OF A CRAPPY THING TO DO.

DOES *BRENDAN* LET YOU USE LANGUAGE LIKE THAT?

YOU — YOU WON'T TELL HIM, WILL YOU?

KID, RELAX. I'M NOT YOUR DAD. SWEAR ALL YOU WANT.

HAHAHA!

HAHAHA! OH, MR. STERLING, YOU'RE HILARIOUS! HOLD ON A SEC.

THMP!

CRASH!

YOU HAVE **DEADLINES.** HAVE YOU FINISHED THAT ASSIGNMENT I GAVE YOU LAST MONTH?

ALMOST. AND I'M WAY AHEAD ON THE INDEPENDENT PROJECT, TOO. CAN'T I WORK ON IT TOMORROW?

YOU'LL WORK ON IT TODAY.

BUT WAIT, WHILE WE'RE TALKING ABOUT IT. I WANTED TO ASK YOU.

ABOUT MY RESEARCH BUDGET.

...CAN I HAVE AN ADVANCE?

SULLA.

I KNOW I KNOW **I KNOW,** BUT JUST A MONTH'S WORTH?

IT'S NOT JUST FOR THE PROJECT, IT'S ALSO FOR PRESENTS.

BIRTHDAY PRESENTS.

FOR YOU.

IT'S **FEBRUARY.** MY BIRTHDAY'S NOT UNTIL —

JULY.

WELL, THEY NEED LOTS OF TIME TO PREPARE! ALL I NEED IS —

WHAT'S UP, LITTLE GUY?

MISS SULLA, GIMEL NEEDS YOU FOR A MOMENT.

HEY.

ALMOST FORGOT. SHE POURED THIS FOR YOU.

OH. GREAT. PERFECT.

THANK YOU.

ATCH - HOT! THAT'S REALLY HOT! DIDN'T THAT HURT YOUR HAND?

I - NO. NO, I GUESS NOT.

OH, RIGHT. RIGHT, OF COURSE NOT.

WHAT SORT OF PROJECTS ARE YOU HAVING HER DO?

ANYTHING SHE WANTS. INDEPENDENT STUDY. IT'S WHAT SHE GETS TO DO INSTEAD OF GOING TO SCHOOL.

SOMETIMES I LET HER FIDDLE WITH AN UNRELEASED STERLING PROTOTYPE AND SEE WHAT SHE CAN DO WITH IT.

YOU'RE STILL PART OF THE COMPANY?

STERLING'S STILL AROUND?

... AL, STERLING INC. IS ONE OF THE BIGGEST ARTIFICIAL INTELLIGENCE DEVELOPERS IN THE UNITED STATES.

I'M THE CEO.

NEW FOR '19 *Sterling*
see who's inside.

FOR NOW, ANYWAY.

I'LL STAY ON AS CHAIRMAN, BUT I'VE BEEN STEPPING AWAY MORE AND MORE OVER THE PAST FEW YEARS.

I NEED TO MAKE TIME FOR MY FAMILY.

NOD NOD NOD

FAMILY.

YES, AL. FAMILY.

IT'S *NICE* HAVING A FAMILY.

I NEED TO MAKE TIME FOR THAT FAMILY.

WHILE I STILL CAN.

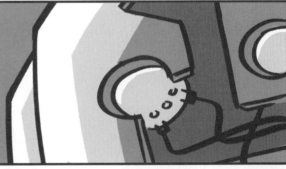

YEAH, I REMEMBER YOU NOW.

CLASS OF '01. CONGRATULATIONS, BY THE WAY.

YOU DID YOUR DISSERTATION ON THE PRACTICAL APPLICATIONS OF *ARTIFICIAL INTELLIGENCE.*

WROTE A CHAT PROGRAM THAT CONVINCED 9 OUT OF 10 USERS THAT THEY WERE TALKING TO A FLIRTATIOUS UNDERGRAD WHO IMPROVISED POETRY ABOUT WHOEVER "SHE" WAS TALKING TO.

THAT'S RIGHT. YOU'VE READ MY PAPERS?

I SKIMMED THEM. THEY WEREN'T BAD.

TODAY YOU'LL BE LABELING WIRES. THERE'S A LABEL GUN FOR YOU TO USE.

I – REALLY?

HAVE FUN.

A – ALL RIGHT. NICE TO FINALLY BE WORKING WITH YOU, MR. STERLING.

AL.

AL.

YEAH, BUT THE STUFF THAT'S ATTACHED THERE RIGHT NOW IS GONNA HAVE TO GO. WE CAN JUST BUY SOME NEW PLATING DOWNTOWN . . .

HEY! MR. STERLING! DO YOU WANT TO GO INTO THE CITY WITH ME?

I—

ABSOLUTELY NOT.

BUT I'M *FINISHED*! ALMOST FINISHED, I NEED TO GO INTO TOWN TO GET SOME MORE SHEET PLATING AND *THEN* I CAN FINISH!

AND MR. STERLING CAN COME WITH. I BET HE'D REALLY LIKE TO SEE EVERYTHING—

UNDER NO CIRCUMSTANCES. THIS ISN'T A GOOD TIME TO GO ON A FIELD TRIP, SULLA, AND YOU KNOW IT.

BUT BRENDAN—

NOBODY'S GOING ANYWHERE TODAY. ESPECIALLY NOT *HIM.*

HEY—

SEE? HE'S BEEN COOPED UP IN THE WORKSHOP ALL NIGHT AND HE HASN'T SEEN HIS HOMETOWN IN SIXTEEN YEARS AND HE'S *LONELY*!

HE'S ALSO AN *ANDROID*. HE WAS ACTIVATED LESS THAN A DAY AGO! THE *FUTURE SHOCK* HE WOULD GET FROM TOO MUCH STIMULATION MIGHT *TRAUMATIZE* HIM PSYCHOLOGICALLY.

WAIT –

IT WON'T *FRY HIS BRAIN* TO GO OUTSIDE, BRENDAN! LET ME TAKE HIM!

LET GO, *BOTH* OF YOU! LET ME OUT OF THIS BASEMENT BEFORE YOU TEAR MY ARMS OFF!

I NEED TO GET OUT OF THIS HOUSE.

AL, IT'S TOO SOON! YOU'LL –

MY BRAIN IS FRYING AS IT IS I'LL TAKE MY CHANCES WITH THE *BACKYARD*

SIR, THE HOUSE SENSORS INDICATE APPROACHING INCLEMENT WEATHER –

MR. STERLING, WE DON'T HAVE TO GO JUST YET...

I DO.

I CAN'T BE AROUND *YOU* AND *HIM* AND... ALL OF *THIS* RIGHT NOW.

WHOOOOOOO

IT WOULD BE IMPRUDENT, GIVEN THE FORECASTED TEMPERATURE OF 22 DEGREES –

WELL, THEN IT'S A GOOD THING I CAN'T *FEEL* IT, HUH?

AT LEAST I WON'T BE *COLD* WHEN I GO OUT INTO THE BIG SCARY –

WHEEEEEE

FINE.

OKAY, WELL, WHEN IT ISN'T SO *GROSS* OUTSIDE, I'LL TAKE YOU INTO TOWN. I CAN INTRODUCE YOU TO THE MACHINISTS I GO TO WHEN I NEED PARTS CUT DOWN OR MODIFIED.

UH HUH.

OH WOW, I BET YOU'VE NEVER EVEN *SEEN* ONE OF THESE ROTORS BEFORE, RIGHT? THEY WERE DEVELOPED IN-HOUSE AT STERLING!

THEY'VE CUT DOW THE POWER LOSSES *SO LO* YOU WOULDN'T *BELIEVE* HO EFFICIENT THEY ARE!

THERE'S THIS ONE GARAGE THAT STOCKS SPECIALIZED ROTORS, RIGHT? AND THEY'RE *MEANT* FOR MONORAIL ENGINES BUT THEY'RE *PERFECT* FOR THE BIG GUY OVER THERE AND —

AND MAKING SURE MACHINES THIS LARGE ARE POWER-EFFICIENT CAN BE *SUCH* A HUGE PROBLEM!

YES, ALL RIGHT. THANKS FOR BEING SO UNDERSTANDING. I'LL CHECK IN LATER. THANK YOU.

BUT, I MEAN, C *COURSE* YOU KNE *THAT.* ALL I MEAN WAS

DON'T TELL ME *YOU'RE* CONFINED TO THE HOUSE, TOO.

SHUF SHUF SHUF

I TOLD MY SECRETARY I WA WORKING FROM HOME TODAY.

AN UNEXPECTED *EMERGENCY* CAME UP AND I HAVE TO TAKE CARE OF IT.

I'LL BE IN MY OFFICE.

YOU DON'T HAVE TO STAY AWAY FROM WORK JUST BECAUSE OF ME —

YEAH, I KNOW.

YOU WANT TO BE LEFT ALONE. I GET IT.

SULLA, LEAVE HIM ALONE IF HE ASKS YOU TO.

OH! SHOULD I — ?

NO, IT'S OKAY. STAY.

TELL ME MORE ABOUT THESE NEW ROTORS.

. . . OKAY.

WELL, YOU KNOW HOW THEY USED TO MAKE THE CONDUCTOR IN STANDARD ROTORS OUT OF ALUMINUM?

WELL, WHAT STERLING DID WAS —

HEY. ASSISTANT.

D'YOU WANT TO ASSIST ME WITH SOMETHING?

WHAT DO YOU NEED?

THIS BIG IDIOT KEEPS STALLING WHEN I RUN HIM THROUGH HIS BASIC TEST SEQUENCE. GETS ALL JERKY.

I CAN'T SPEND THE REST OF THE MORNING PICKING THROUGH HIS CORE PROGRAMMING FOR *BUGS*.

CAN YOU TAKE CARE OF THIS?

SURE, IT SEEMS EASY ENOUGH. I CAN RUN A FEW SOFTWARE TESTS OF MY OWN AND SEE WHERE THE PROBLEM IS. IT SHOULDN'T TAKE MORE THAN AN HOUR.

TAK TAK TAK

AN *HOUR*.

NOT EVEN THAT.

THAT'S QUITE A PROMISE.

I'M GOOD AT FIXING THINGS.

I'LL KEEP YOU TO THAT. KNOW WHAT'LL HAPPEN IF YOU TAKE MORE THAN AN HOUR?

NO. WHAT'LL HAPPEN?

YOU'LL BE IN *TROUBLE*.

REALLY? WHAT'RE YOU GONNA DO?

I'LL THINK OF SOMETHING. IT'LL BE PRETTY BAD.

heh.

HMPH.

THE HELL IS HE DOING.

THE HELL ARE YOU DOING?

I TOLD YOU IT WAS JUST A *SOFTWARE BUG.* YOU DON'T NEED TO BE IN THERE.

YEAH, BUT I HAD AN IDEA. I DON'T THINK IT'S A SOFTWARE PROBLEM. IT'S *MECHANICAL.*

I THINK A FEW OF THE ROTORS DON'T TURN WHEN THE SEQUENCE RUNS, SO THE BRAIN GETS CONFUSED AND GIVES AN ERROR MESSAGE WHEN THE ENGINE DOESN'T RESPOND.

ARE THE ROTORS STUCK? DID YOU CLEAN THEM?

YUP, DID THAT.

AND THE WIRING ISN'T SHOT?

UH-UH.

WHAT ABOUT CHANGING THE VOLTAGE TOLERANCES ON EACH OF THE ROTORS YOURSELF? THEY SHOULD HAVE LITTLE *CHIPS* ON 'EM . . . MAYBE THEY NEED TO BE TWEAKED.

I, UH . . . DIDN'T KNOW HOW TO DO THAT. I WAS GONNA WAIT UNTIL YOU WERE DONE TO ASK.

I'M FREE NOW. MOVE OVER.

YOU DID A PRETTY GOOD JOB ON THE SOLDERING IN HERE. DIDN'T KNOW THEY STILL TAUGHT UNDERGRAD KIDS HOW TO HANDLE STUFF LIKE THIS.

YIKES. WE'RE *KIDS* TO YOU? YOU DIDN'T SEEM *THAT* OLD.

LOTS OF PEOPLE ARE KIDS TO ME. LOTS OF *THIRTY-SOMETHINGS* ACT LIKE KIDS.

NOTHING PERSONAL. THE FACT THAT I HAVEN'T HAD TO BABYSIT YOU ALREADY PUTS YOU PRETTY HIGH UP IN MY BOOK.

THANKS, I GUESS. BUT I DIDN'T REALLY LEARN ANY OF THIS STUFF AT MIT.

NO?

WHEN I WAS A KID – AN *ACTUAL* KID – I OWNED THIS REALLY ADVANCED CIRCUITRY SET. I LOVED IT. IT WAS GREAT SEEING HOW STUFF CONNECTED TOGETHER LIKE THAT, FROM THE INSIDE.

THINGS GO SO MUCH MORE SMOOTHLY WHEN YOU START OFF KNOWING EXACTLY *HOW* IT'LL WORK AND WHAT YOU WANT IT TO *DO*. AND IT DOESN'T JUST GO FOR MACHINES, EITHER. EVERY PROJECT NEEDS A GOOD FRAMEWORK TO BUILD FROM.

I'VE HAD THESE PLANS FOR A COMPANY – A REAL *SOFTWARE COMPANY* – THAT I CAN START UP WITHIN THREE YEARS. I'VE BEEN PLANNING IT OUT SINCE I WAS *SIXTEEN*.

A COMPANY, HUH? YOU'RE AMBITIOUS.

WHAT'LL YOU DO WHEN THE COMPANY FAILS?

THAT'S – PRETTY CYNICAL.

EVERYBODY FAILS, BRENDAN. LEARNING HOW TO FAIL IS PRETTY IMPORTANT, TOO.

YOU LOOK LIKE YOU KNOW HOW TO LEARN FROM FAILURE, THOUGH. THAT'S GOOD.

THAT'S WHAT ADULTS DO.

ALL RIGHT. TAKE A LOOK AT WHAT I DID WITH THE ROTOR HERE. MAKE SENSE?

IS THAT ALL THERE IS TO IT?

CAN – CAN YOU SHOW ME ONE MORE TIME?

YOU GOT IT.

NORTH5

HEY, AL!

I GOT US SOMETHING OVER AT THAT SANDWICH PLACE DOWN THE STREET.

YOU DID?

YEAH. IT'S HALF PAST THREE AND I HAVEN'T SEEN YOU EAT OR . . . NOT WORK.

OH. THANKS. I'LL PAY YOU BACK –

AL.

YOU'RE NOT SERIOUSLY EATING ALONE, ARE YOU?

SO.

UH.

HOW'S WORK ON GIMEL 49 GOING?

OH, FINE! JUST FINE. THE PROBLEM WAS WHAT WE THOUGHT.

GIMEL'S SUCH A BIG THING, ALL OF THE WEIGHT IS PUTTING TOO MUCH STRESS ON THE MOTORS. THAT'S WHY IT COULDN'T RUN A COMPLETE MOTION CYCLE.

FINE.

THAT'S FINE.

SO WHO'S CONTRACTING YOU TO DESIGN THE GIMEL PROTOTYPES, ANYWAY? AND WHAT ABOUT THOSE LITTLE ROBOTS, THE BETHS?

NO ONE. THEY'RE ALL PERSONAL PROJECTS. EXPERIMENTS.

ARE YOU SERIOUS?

I TOL' YOU THA' THE CONTRAC' WORK WAS COMING IN LITTLE SLOW LATEL' I THOUGHT YOU DIDN' CARE WHAT THE WOR' WAS LIKE. I THOUGH' YOU JUST WANTE' TO WORK HER'

I DON'T CARE ABOUT THE CONTRACTS! THIS IS ALL JUST FOR YOU? THAT HUGE ROBOT IS JUST FOR YOU?

ANY OF MY MIT PROFESSORS WOULD TRADE AN ARM TO WORK WITH ONE OF THOSE PROTOTYPES! YOU SERIOUSLY HAVEN'T HAD ANYONE CALL ABOUT SOME OF THIS STUFF?

THIS MAY SURPRISE YOU, BUT I'M NOT REALLY THE HOT RESEARCHER ON THE ROBOTICS CIRCUIT YOU'RE CONFUSING ME FOR. I DON'T GET CALLS.

AND THE COMPETITION FOR YOUR JOB WASN'T EXACTLY STIFF.

I FIND THAT HARD TO BELIEVE.

ANYWAY, THERE'S NOT MUCH HERE TO INTEREST MOST OF THE ROBOT PEOPLE.

I DON'T BELIEVE THAT, EITHER. I'VE SEEN THE WAY YOU WORK WITH THEM.

THE ROBOTICISTS?

THE ROBOTS. YOU **SEE** SOMETHING IN THEM. YOU TREAT THEM DIFFERENTLY.

THEY AREN'T JUST TOOLS AND – AND GLORIFIED **CHAT PROGRAMS** TO YOU. YOU DESIGN THEM AS IF THEY CAN BE **MORE** THAN THAT.

THEY **CAN** BE MORE. THEY **SHOULD** BE. MOST OF US HAVE BARELY SCRATCHED THE SURFACE WHEN IT COMES TO FINDING OUT HOW MUCH ROBOTS CAN DO.

ARTIFICIAL INTELLIGENCES CAN **OBSERVE** AND **PREDICT**, BUT THEY CAN **THINK** AND **CREATE**, TOO. AI'S HAVE THE POTENTIAL TO BE . . . PRACTICALLY HUMAN. MAYBE EVEN SUPERHUMAN.

BUT WE HAVEN'T LET THEM.

BECAUSE WE DON'T HAVE THE RESOURCES TO MAKE IT HAPPEN?

NO.

WE **DON'T** LET THEM. IT'S **FEAR**.

WE'RE **SCARED** OF WHAT THEY CAN BE. ROBOTICISTS MORE THAN ANYONE ELSE. BECAUSE WE KNOW **EXACTLY** HOW MUCH THINGS CAN CHANGE.

IF WE LET THEM.

WHAT ARE YOU DOING?

YOU'RE RIGHT. YOU'RE ABSOLUTELY RIGHT. ROBOTS CAN BE SO MUCH MORE.

WE SHOULD START MAKING THEM RIGHT NOW.

WHAT? NO. I WAS RAMBLING.

BRENDAN, LISTEN, EVEN IF PEOPLE WERE SUDDENLY OKAY WITH MACHINES THAT COULD THINK – *ACTUALLY* THINK – WE'RE YEARS, *DECADES* FROM SEEING ANY REAL DEVELOPMENT IN THE TECHNOLOGY.

WE STILL CAN'T FIGURE OUT HOW *HUMAN* BRAINS FUNCTION, LET ALONE TRY TO RE-CREATE THAT PROCESS IN A *DIGITAL* BRAIN.

WHY BUILD A BRAIN FROM SCRATCH? THE HUMAN BRAIN'S ALREADY AN ELECTRIC-POWERED DIGITAL *MACHINE.*

EVERY FIRING SYNAPSE IS A BIT TURNING ON AND OFF. WE JUST NEED TO . . . *TRANSLATE* THAT BINARY INTO ONE WE CAN UNDERSTAND. TO TURN AN ORGANIC BRAIN INTO A *PROGRAM.* A LEGIBLE DIGITAL DOCUMENT.

AND ONCE WE HAVE IT, IT'S JUST A MATTER OF PRESSING *CONTROL-C.* YOU CAN *DUPLICATE* HUMAN BEINGS.

YEAH, BUT.

IT'S ONLY A COPY FROM THAT *INITIAL POINT.*

WHATEVER THE COPY DOES *AFTER* THAT, WHATEVER THAT BRAIN *SAYS* OR *THINKS* OR *MAKES*, CAN BE COMPLETELY DIFFERENT FROM WHAT THE ORIGINAL GOES ON TO DO.

BUT BY THAT LOGIC, THOSE BRAINS BECOME LESS AND LESS IDENTICAL OVER TIME. THEY AREN'T *COPIES* ANYMORE. THEY'RE –

PEOPLE. INDIVIDUAL PEOPLE.

AUTONOMOUS –

– ARTIFICIAL –

– PEOPLE.

~CRRMPL~

IT'S FOUR O'CLOCK. GO HOME. I'LL PAY YOU BACK FOR THE SANDWICH TOMORROW.

OH! IS – IS THAT ALL FOR TODAY?

YEAH. GO HOME, BRENDAN.

TAP
TAP
TAP
TAP

HEY, THAT'S COOL! WHAT'S THAT FOR, AL?

SHOVE

NOTHING. NOTHING. JUST A SIDE PROJECT.

WHERE'RE YOU AT ON THE BIG ROBOT'S CALIBRATIONS?

I THOUGHT I SHOWED YOU YESTERDAY — IT'S JUST ANOTHER AFTERNOON'S WORTH OF WORK AND WE CAN HAVE IT RUN THROUGH ITS MOTION CYCLE.

THAT'S FINE. I'M GOING ON A SUPPLY RUN. YOU GO AHEAD AND . . . DO THAT.

DO YOU NEED ANY HELP, OR —

NO. NO, JUST — I NEED TO BE BY MYSELF FOR A WHILE. FINISH THE CALIBRATIONS.

O — OKAY. IS THAT ALL —

YES.

YES, THAT IS ALL.

TAP
TAP
TAP
TAP

I THINK THE STORM'S STARTING TO BLOW OVER.

WE CAN PROBABLY GO OUT LATER –

I MEAN, UNLESS YOU WANTED TO GO ON YOUR *OWN* . . .

NO, WE CAN GO TOGETHER. LATER.

I JUST NEED TO TAKE A WALK OR SOMETHING FIRST. THERE'S A LOT OF STUFF BOTHERING ME.

IS THAT WHY YOU'RE PICKING AT YOUR SHIRT?

YOU DO THE SAME THING I DO. YOU PICK AT THINGS.

YOU SHOULDN'T PICK AT YOUR SHIRT. THAT'S THE ONLY ONE YOU *HAVE*.

WHY ARE YOU ANGRY AT BRENDAN?

I NEVER SAID I WAS.

YOU *ARE*, THOUGH.

WOULDN'T YOU BE?

BEING . . . BROUGHT BACK LIKE THIS?

DIDN'T YOU WANT TO BE? I MEAN, I THOUGHT THAT'S WHAT YOU *WANTED* HIM TO DO. WHY ARE YOU ANGRY?

I THOUGHT YOU WERE BEST FRIENDS.

HE SAID THAT.

. . . YEAH.

YEAH, WELL.

EVEN BEST FRIENDS MAKE MISTAKES.

WHERE IS IT?

WHERE IS IT?!

OFFICE.

IT MUST BE IN THE OFFICE. IT HAS TO BE.

YOU WHAT.

I - I JUST *TWEAKED* THE CODE A LITTLE. I SAW IT OPEN ON THE LAPTOP AFTER YOU LEFT AND I KNEW IT WAS GIVING YOU TROUBLE, SO I -

WHAT GAVE YOU *ANY* RIGHT TO TOUCH THAT?

YOU HAD *EVERYTHING* ELSE TO MESS AROUND WITH IN THIS WORKSHOP AND YOU *STILL* -

I DIDN'T OVERWRITE ANY OF THE ORIGINAL CODE, AL, IT'S ALL STILL THERE. I JUST -

THAT DOESN'T MATTER.

THAT ROBOT WAS THE ONLY THING THAT DIDN'T -

GET OUT. YOU'RE GONE. I'LL MAIL YOU THE LAST PAYCHECK, BUT YOU NEED TO -

NO.

AL, IT'S PRETTY OBVIOUS THAT THIS ISN'T ABOUT THE DANCER.

BUT . . .

SINCE YOU DON'T WANT TO TALK ABOUT *THAT*, LET'S KEEP IT ABOUT THE DANCER.

I'M SORRY IF I STEPPED OUT OF BOUNDS BY EDITING THE CODE. I REALLY AM.

I KNOW THIS PROJECT MEANS A LOT TO YOU AND I WASN'T TRYING TO – TO SABOTAGE IT.

YOU'RE AN INCREDIBLY TALENTED INVENTOR – NO – YOU'RE A *GENIUS*. I'M SURE YOU KNEW WHAT YOU WERE DOING.

BUT. I DON'T TRY SOMETHING UNLESS I'M SURE I KNOW WHAT *I'M* DOING.

LOOK, I KNOW I DON'T KNOW HOW TO *FAIL*, OR WHATEVER, BUT I'M PRETTY GOOD AT EVERYTHING ELSE. I'M *REALLY* GOOD AT WHAT I DO.

I – OH, JEEZ. GOD, I'M SORRY. I'M ALREADY FIRED. I SHOULD JUST –

NO.

I'M LISTENING.

I REALLY ADMIRE YOU. I HAVE FOR A WHILE NOW. THE WHOLE TIME I'VE BEEN HERE, I'VE BEEN IN *AWE*. IT'S BEEN AMAZING JUST TO WATCH HOW YOUR MIND WORKS.

AL ...

I WANT TO BE HERE. I WANT TO SEE WHAT HAPPENS NEXT FOR YOU.

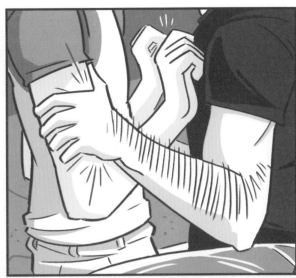

SSSHF

CHIRRUP
CHIRRUP
CHIRP

☀ 10/2/01
SUNNY... 65°

SH.

NICE BEDHEAD.

FFFGGHH.

WHAT WAS *THAT* FOR?

NAH, NOTHING. IT'S JUST – YEAH, MY HAIR. AND MY FACE.

YOUR FACE.

MY BEARD. I NEED TO SHAVE IT. I JUST REALIZED I'D FORGOTTEN TO SHAVE THIS WHOLE WEEK.

WHAT? NO!

I'VE BEEN A MESS ALL WEEK, AND IT SHOWS. HELL, YOU SAW WHAT A MESS I WAS LAST NIGHT –

AL –

AL.

YOU LOOK *FINE*. YOU *DID* FINE. LISTEN, WHEN I SLEPT WITH A GU FOR THE FIRST TIME, HE HAD TO SHOW ME HOW TO DO *EVERYTHING*. YOU'RE A MUCH FASTER LEARNER THAN I WAS.

SO DID I PASS?

YOU DID MORE THAN *PASS*.

AND FOR YOUR INFORMATION...

THE BEARD WAS THE BEST PART.

KEEP IT LIKE THIS.

D'YOU WANT TO SHOWER BEFORE WE GET BACK TO WORK?

WORK? WE'RE **WORKING** TODAY?

WE'RE RUNNING THE BIG GUY'S MOTION CYCLE TODAY, REMEMBER? THE SYSTEMS CHECK FINISHED LAST NIGHT. IT SHOULD BE GOOD TO GO!

YOU SURE THAT'S WHAT YOU WANT TO DO **FIRST**?

SEX CAN **WAIT**! SCIENTIFIC BREAKTHROUGHS HAPPEN **NOW**!

ALL RIGHT, ALL RIGHT.

HA HA

RUN PROGRAM

WHRRRRRRRRR

CLICK CLICK

CLICK

CLICK
CLICK
CLICK
CLICK

PULL IT WITH ME.

CLUNK

I GOT THIS. GO AHEAD AND TURN HIM OFF.

O - OKAY.

SMAK

CLUNK
CLUNK
CLUN
CLUNK
CLUNK

HA.

HA HA HA HA HA

MAN!

HA HA HA

WE GOTTA START MAKING THEM SMALLER.

ARE YOU OKAY?

BRENDAN...

WHAT'S WRONG?

THIS IS A – ...

WE CAN'T DO THIS. WE CAN'T MAKE THIS WORK. THIS IS SUCH A BAD IDEA FOR SO MANY REASONS.

WHAT ARE THEY?

I'M SERIOUS. GIVE ME YOUR REASONS.

FOR STARTERS, WE'V'̶ GOT A JOB TO DO. WE'L̶ BE AROUND EACH OTHE̶ ALL THE TIME̶

I'M SURE TWO GROWN MEN CAN FIGURE OUT HOW TO BUDGET THEIR TIME.

WE'RE GOING TO DRIVE EACH OTHER CRAZY.

I'M SUR̶ WE WIL̶ WHAT ELSE̶

BRENDAN, LOOK AT ME. THIS ISN'T WHAT GUYS YOUR AGE WANT. I'M TOO OLD FOR YOU. YOU DON'T WANT THIS.

KEEP GOING.

I DON'T KNOW HOW TO DO THIS.

I - I DON'T HAVE ANY IDEA WHAT I'M DOING.

I DO.

LET ME BE THE KNOW-IT-ALL FOR THIS, OKAY? TRUST ME.

THIS ISN'T A MISTAKE.

DON'T THINK WE'RE GETTING ANY MORE WORK DONE TODAY.

NOPE.

WELCOME

ARTIFICIAL
INTELLIGENCE
DEVELOP

HEY.

HEY. IS THE TV TOO LOUD?

NO, IT'S – CAN'T YOU SLEEP?

THERE WAS TOO MUCH ON MY MIND. WORKING ON THIS HELPS ME THINK.

WELL, AS LONG AS YOU'RE IN THE MOOD FOR THINKING...

SINCE NOVEMBER'S ALMOST OVER, MAYBE WE CAN THINK ABOUT WHAT WE WANT TO DO...

...Y'KNOW, FOR THE HOLIDAYS.

I USUALLY SPEND A WEEK OR TWO AT MY PARENTS' HOUSE AND –

I KNOW YOU'RE NOT RELIGIOUS AND YOU DON'T HAVE TO DO THE HANUKKAH THING.

BUT YOUR BIRTHDAY'S COMING UP, TOO. WE CAN CELEBRATE WITH THEM.

YOU CAN BE MY "FRIEND." BUT THEY WOULDN'T CARE. YOU KNOW –

I'LL THINK ABOUT IT.

NOW THAT I THINK ABOUT IT –

I MEAN, WHAT DO *YOU* USUALLY DO? DO YOU VISIT *YOUR* FOLKS, OR –

OH! THE A5 CON-NECTOR BROKE. LEMME GET A SPARE.

I GOT IT.

I DON'T REALLY... KEEP IN TOUCH WITH MY FAMILY.

WHAT — AT ALL?

WHEN I WAS IN HIGH SCHOOL I WAS RAISED BY AN AUNT AND UNCLE.

THEY WERE ALL RIGHT — I MADE SURE THEY DIDN'T HAVE TO DO MUCH FOR ME. ONCE I GOT AN ENGINEER-ING SCHOLARSHIP I GOT OUT OF THEIR WAY.

BUT BEFORE THAT, YOU LIVED WITH YOUR PARENTS?

I HAVEN'T TALKED TO MY PARENTS IN A LONG TIME. IT'S BETTER THAT WAY.

WERE YOU — CAN I ASK WHAT HAPPENED?

GO BACK TO SLEEP, BRENDAN.

IN ROBOTICS, A RISING STAR!

2011 STERLIN

AI-CON 2002

THD
THMPT

THD

THMPT

SHF SHF

SHFFF

WHAT'RE YOU LOOKING FOR?

GAH!

SKRITCH SKRITCH

DON'T *SCARE* ME LIKE THAT!

JUST... LEAVE ME ALONE, ALL RIGHT? I'M BUSY.

DOING WHAT?

IT'S - IT'S NONE OF YOUR CONCERN, AL. LEAVE ME BE.

NONE OF MY CONCERN.

OKAY.

OH, *PLEASE.* DON'T GET LIKE THAT.

I'M HAVING A *VERY*

FRUS-TRATING

DAY RIGHT NOW.

AND THE LAST THING I NEED IS *ATTITUDE* FROM THE *GHOST OF HANUKKAH PAST*

SO IF YOU COULD JUST –

...

WHERE DID YOU GET THAT?

AS I RECALL, IT WAS A *BIRTHDAY PRESENT,* BRENDAN.

HOW THE *HELL* DID YOU GET YOUR MULTITOOL BACK? YOU *CAN'T* HAVE – THERE'S NO *WAY.*

IT'S *MINE.*

DON'T PULL THAT WITH ME. ONLY I KNEW WHERE I KEPT IT. YOU *COULDN'T* HAVE FOUND IT.

I WOKE UP WITH IT IN MY POCKET. *YOU* OUGHT TO KNOW THAT, SEEING AS YOU *PUT* IT THERE.

YOU DON'T STILL THINK I –

AL, YOU *DIED.* I THOUGHT YOU WERE *GONE.*

WHY *WOULDN'T* YOU GIVE THIS BACK TO ME? MAKES IT A PERFECT PICTURE, DOESN'T IT?

STOP IT.

REALLY COMPLETES THE WHOLE THING.

I TOLD YOU, I DIDN'T BRING YOU BACK –

REALLY.

THEN WHY DO YOU CARE ABOUT THIS SO MUCH? WHO IS THIS FOR?

YOU'RE NOT SUPPOSED TO HAVE THE MULTI-TOOL ANYMORE –

I WAS SAVING IT FOR *SULLA!*

111

I WAS GOING TO GIVE HER THE MULTITOOL.

FOR HER SIXTEENTH BIRTHDAY.

YOU DIDN'T DO IT.

AND *NOW* HE LISTENS.

BUT IF YOU DIDN'T –   THEN WHO –

I DON'T KNOW. I DON'T KNOW.

THIS DOESN'T MAKE *ANY SENSE!* WHO *WAS* IT, IF IT WASN'T YOU?

IF YOU COULDN'T BE BOTHERED TO –

YOU THINK I DIDN'T *WANT* YOU BACK? YOU THINK I DIDN'T TRY *EVERYTHING I COULD THINK OF* TO KEEP YOU WITH ME?!

I MADE A COPY BECAUSE I *COULD.* AND BECAUSE I WAS *DESPERATE.*

BUT I COULDN'T COPY YOU RIGHT THE *FIRST* TIME. WITH YOU RIGHT THERE IN FRONT OF ME IN THE HOSPITAL BED.

WHAT MAKES YOU THINK I COULD GET IT RIGHT *NOW?*

... HEY, KIDDO.

I - I'M SORRY! I DIDN'T MEAN TO - BUT I JUST HEARD MY NAME AND...

SOME YELLING...

ARE YOU LEAVING?

HE'S NOT LEAVING. NOBODY'S LEAVING.

AL AND I... *AGREED*... THAT NEITHER OF US ARE DIRECTLY RESPONSIBLE FOR HIM BEING HERE. BUT I'M MAKING IT MY RESPONSIBILITY TO FIND OUT WHERE HE CAME FROM.

IN THE MEANTIME, HOWEVER, HE IS MORE THAN WELCOME TO STAY HERE.

ALASTAIR IS ONE OF THE BEST FRIENDS THAT I'VE EVER HAD REGARDLESS OF THE *CIRCUMSTANCES* THAT HAVE BROUGHT HIM BACK...

HE'S BACK.

AND WE SHOULD BE HERE FOR HIM.

I'LL HAVE TO SET UP A BETTER BED FOR YOU DOWN IN THE WORKSHOP.

I CAN DO IT!

WE CAN REBUILD THE DAY BED!

YOU DON'T HAVE TO DO THAT —

GO AHEAD AND HELP HER OUT. I HAVE A FEW PHONE CALLS TO MAKE.

COME ONNNN. MR. STERLING! WE GOTTA GET MY TOOLS TOGETHER!

ALL RIGHT, ALL RIGHT.

I'VE GOT THIS.

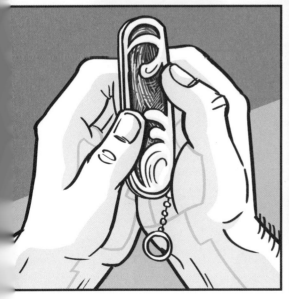

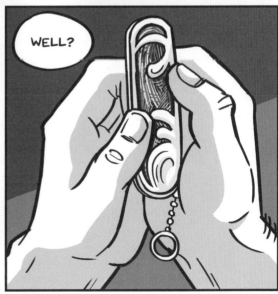

WELL?

DO YOU LIKE IT?

IT'S GOT ALL OF THE TOOLS YOU USE ON A DAILY BASIS, SO YOU WON'T HAVE TO TURN OVER THE WORKSHOP TO FIND YOUR PHILLIPS-HEAD ANY MORE.

IS THIS MOTHER-OF-PEARL ON THE HANDLE?

I ORDERED THAT PART SPECIAL. IT SEEMED LIKE YOUR KIND OF THING.

THIS IS AMAZING, BRENDAN.

FLIK

YOU DESERVE IT! I MEAN, IT'S NOT JUST A HA

NO

NUKKAH PRESENT, IT'S YOUR

DON'T SAY IT

BIRTHDAY PRESENT TOO —

NO WHY DID YOU SAY IT

WHY DID YOU MAKE ME REMEMBER.

I'M FORTY NOW.

JEEZ.

HEY, NO MOPING. WE AREN'T MOPING.

"IN THE MORNING I'D AWAKE,
AND I COULDN'T REMEMBER.
WHAT IS LOVE AND WHAT IS HATE?
THE CALCULATIONS ERROR.
IS TO LOVE JUST A WASTE?
AND HOW CAN IT MATTER?"

- THE FLAMING LIPS,
IN THE MORNING OF THE MAGICIANS
2002

CHAPTER THREE
Mansions for the Soul

DID YOU GET TO SEE THAT THEATER ON THE RIVER LAST TIME YOU WERE HERE, MR. STERLING?

THE FOSHAY! I BET YOU HAVEN'T BEEN TO THE TOP OF THE FOSHAY YET!

WHAT ABOUT THE SKYWAYS? WE COULD TAKE YOU THROUGH THE SKYWAYS.

SULLA, THE FOSHAY'S ALMOST A HUNDRED YEARS OLD. IT'S NOT EVEN THE TALLEST SKYSCRAPER IN THE CITY ANYMORE.

BUT IT'S GOT AN OBSERVATION DECK! IT'D BE A GOOD WAY TO SEE EVERYTHING THAT'S DIFFERENT NOW.

CAN'T SAY I WENT THERE WHEN I WAS ALIVE.

I KNOW WHERE WE CAN GO! YOU WOULDN'T HAVE SEEN THE CENTRAL LIBRARY DOWN-TOWN, WOULD YOU? I MEAN, I WAS A COUPLE YEARS OLD WHEN THEY FINISHED IT.

A LIBRARY. ONE OF THE STOPS ON MY GRAND TOUR IS GONNA BE A LIBRARY.

YEAH, BUT IT'S HUGE! AND IT'S GOT THIS BIG THING ON TOP, AND –

TAKE IT EASY ON THE SIGHT-SEEING, OKAY? I STILL NEED HIM TO COME UP TO STERLING SOMETIME TODAY.

CAN'T IT WAIT 'TIL LATER? I DON'T WANT HIM TO SIT IN A BOARDROOM ALL DAY.

LET'S GET GOING, MR. STERLING! WE'LL BE BACK IN A FEW HOURS!

LOOK AFTER HIM, SWEETHEART. THIS IS A BIG CHANGE FOR HIM.

I PROMISE. WE'LL HAVE FUN.

STERLING PLAZA

WELL
. . .

I GUESS BRENDAN WAS RIGHT. IT WAS PROBABLY TOO MUCH AT ONCE.

ONCE YOU GET USED TO EVERYTHING, YOU'LL BE OKAY. IN THE MEANTIME, *LEM'S* IS A GOOD PLACE TO RELAX.

IT'S SAFE HERE, Y'KNOW?

I THINK I'M GONNA GET A SNACK FOR BRENDAN.

124

THEY'RE LOOKING AT ME.

EVERY ROBOT IN HERE HAS TRIED LOOKING AT ME AT LEAST ONCE.

DO THEY RECOGNIZE ME?

I WOULDN'T WORRY ABOUT IT. THEY CAN TELL YOU'RE *SYNTHETIC*. I DON'T THINK THEY KNOW ANY MORE THAN THAT.

THEY CAN?

WELL, YEAH.

YOU KNOW, MR. STERLING, WE'RE BOTH REALLY *LUCKY*.

THERE'S A LOT YOU CAN *CHANGE* ABOUT YOURSELF WHEN YOU'RE SYNTHETIC. THERE'S THIS KIND OF *FREEDOM* THAT ORGANIC PEOPLE DON'T REALLY HAVE FROM THE START.

YOU CAN LOOK HOWEVER YOU WANT. WHATEVER SUITS YOU BEST.

BUT TO LOOK *HUMAN* – PASSABLY HUMAN, I MEAN – TAKES TECHNOLOGY THAT'S STILL SUPER-DUPER EXPENSIVE. I CAN LOOK THE WAY I WANT TO LOOK BECAUSE, WELL, *BRENDAN*. AND YOU... WHO KNOWS?

BUT MOST OF THE OTHERS CAN'T REALLY AFFORD TO LOOK LIKE US YET.

SYNTHETIC PEOPLE, WE CAN SPOT EACH OTHER. WE KNOW WHAT TO LOOK FOR.

BUT MOST *ORGANIC* PEOPLE WOULD PROBABLY NEVER REALIZE THERE WAS ANYTHING THAT MADE ME DIFFERENT FROM ANY OTHER GIRL.

AND I GUESS THERE'S A KIND OF FREEDOM IN THAT, TOO.

YOU KNOW, I NEVER WOULD HAVE GUESSED. YOU PASS REALLY WELL.

FOR REAL?

YEAH. IF IT WEREN'T FOR THE FLYING, YOU WOULD LOOK POSITIVELY HUMAN.

I – OH, HUMAN. OH.

WELL, BRENDAN'S BEEN WORKING ON ME FOR SO LONG THAT I GUESS HE'S MADE ME LOOK...

CONVINCING.

WELL, IT WORKS. YOU COULD PASS FOR ANY REGULAR SIXTEEN-YEAR-OLD GIRL I'VE EVER SEEN.

FIFTEEN.

HEY, YOUR HAND! HOW'D THAT CUT GET THERE?

HUH? OH. I JUST WANTED TO SEE WHAT IT LOOKED LIKE, YOU KNOW, UNDERNEATH.

IT LOOKS PRETTY MUCH LIKE YOU'D EXPECT. IF YOU'RE BUILT LIKE ME, I MEAN. ADVANCED SYNTHETIC MUSCLES AND STUFF LOOK A LOT LIKE THE REAL THING.

YOU SHOULD GET BRENDAN TO LOOK AT IT TODAY. HE'LL PROBABLY TRY TO POKE AROUND IN THERE, ANYWAY.

"POKE AROUND."

WELL, THAT'S NOTHING HE HASN'T TRIED ALREADY.

OH, HE'S ALREADY EXAMINED YOU. THAT'S GOOD.

YOU MEAN HE HASN'T TOLD YOU —

TOLD ME WHAT?

OH, DON'T BE NERVOUS ABOUT GOING TO *STERLING* TODAY! I THINK HE JUST WANTS TO GIVE HIS FRIEND THE *TOUR*, Y'KNOW?

NEVER MIND.

UGH, GOD.

WHAT'S WRONG?

GUH, *SWEET*. WAY TOO SWEET. IS EVERYTHING I'M GOING TO EAT FROM NOW ON MADE OUT OF *FRUCTOSE*?

PRETTY MUCH. SORRY.

WHY?

WELL, IT'S ENGINEERED TO BE EFFICIENTLY BROKEN DOWN BY SYNTHETIC SYSTEMS SO THEY CAN —

BECAUSE *PEOPLE* DO THEM.

NO, I MEAN EATING. SLEEPING. DO WE *CRAP* NOW, TOO? WHY MAKE ROBOTS WHO HAVE TO DO *PEOPLE* THINGS?

WHAT IS IT?

I JUST REALIZED THAT I'LL NEVER GET TO HAVE SRIRACHA AGAIN.

SRI—

OH, THE SAUCE WITH THE *ROOSTER* ON THE BOTTLE? BRENDAN TOLD ME YOU *LOVED* SPICY STUFF.

YEAH.

YEAH, I DID.

YOU DIDN'T ANSWER MY OTHER QUESTION.

SORRY. WHAT WAS IT?

DO ROBOTS *CRAP* NOW, TOO?

NOT IF YOU KEEP EATING FRUCTOSE.

- REST.

GREAT. 'CAUSE I'VE GOT ABOUT A BAJILLION FORMS THAT NEED YOUR SIGNATURE BEFORE I MAIL THEM OUT.

READY TO TAKE A BREAK FROM WORKING ON THAT?

YEAH. SURE, I COULD USE A -

IT NEVER STOPS, DOES IT.

RUNNING A COMPANY MEANS FILING *PAPERWORK,* AL. THAT'S HOW IT GOES.

DON'T REMEMBER DOING *HALF* AS MUCH THE LAST TIME I TRIED THIS.

LAST TIME, STERLING *TANKED.* WE GOTTA PUT ALL OF OUR EFFORTS INTO THIS IF OTHER PEOPLE ARE GONNA TAKE OUR PROTOTYPES *SERIOUSLY.*

THE CONFER-ENCE.

. . . WILL HELP WITH THAT, YES. POTENTIAL INVESTORS NEED TO SEE WHAT OUR PRODUCTS CAN DO IN A LIVE DEMONSTRATION. WE NEED TO MAKE SURE OUR PRODUCTS CAN *SURPRISE* THEM . . .

AND THE NEURON EMULATOR CAN DO THAT.

I KNOW IT CAN.

IF WE CAN GET FUNDING FOR THE EMULATOR AND THE BODY PROTOTYPES, WE'LL HAVE OPPORTUNITIES WE DIDN'T HAVE BEFORE.

WE CAN MOVE PRODUCTION OUT OF OUR WORKSHOP. WE CAN HIRE A PERMANENT STAFF. I CAN EVEN GET A CUTE SECRETARY TO DO ALL THE PAPERWORK.

I ALREADY *HAVE* A CUTE SECRETARY.

ASS.

ARE YOU *KIDDING* ME?

YOU CAN'T WORK ON THIS *NOW!* THE EMULATOR'S *OS* NEEDS TO BE DEBUGGED BY *FRIDAY!* IF THE ROBOT RUNS INTO AN ERROR MESSAGE IN THE MIDDLE OF THE DEMO—

JUNE 20 02

IF THE ROBOT CAN'T *WALK* PROPERLY, THEN IT WON'T MATTER IF IT GETS AN ERROR MESSAGE OR NOT. *EVERYTHING* NEEDS TO BE DONE BY FRIDAY.

I KNOW. AAAGH. WHAT IF THIS DOESN'T WORK?

LOOK, JUST STOP FOR A SECOND AND THINK THIS THROUGH.

THINK ABOUT WHETHER ALL THESE THINGS YOU'VE BEEN PLANNING ARE THINGS WE CAN ACTUALLY GET *DONE.*

IT'S NOT THE END OF THE WORLD IF WE AREN'T READY FOR THIS YET.

WE CAN TRY AGAIN NEXT YEAR.

NO. THIS IS DOABLE. THERE'S A LOT OF STUFF TO FINISH, BUT IF WE TOUGH IT OUT, WE CAN BE READY IN TIME.

WELL, OKAY, THEN. TELL ME WHAT YOU NEED ME TO DO AND I'LL SEE THAT IT'S DONE.

SKRK

TWITCH TWITCH

SKRK

ERROR

Unable to connect to operating system.

OK

6/21
HAS OS
BEEN
DEBUG

JUNE

20
02

YOU STILL NERVOUS?

I'LL BE ABLE TO **SLEEP**, AT LEAST. I MEAN, AT THIS POINT THERE'S NOT MUCH MORE WE CAN DO, RIGHT?

WHATEVER'S GONNA HAPPEN IS GONNA HAPPEN. YOU'VE DONE PLENTY TO READY FOR THIS THING.

WE'VE DONE PLENTY. NONE OF THIS WOULD HAVE BEEN POSSIBLE WITHOUT YOU.

IT WOULD BE PERFECT IF...

IF YOU COULD HOLD MY HAND TOMORROW. IF I COULD SHOW EVERYONE HOW MUCH YOU MEAN TO ME.

BUT.

I UNDER-TAND WHY OU **CAN'T**.

IT'S FINE. WE'LL DO FINE.

I HAVEN'T SEEN YOU SINCE THE PARTY IN NOVEMBER!

YOU'RE LOOKING SHARP!

IT'S GOOD TO SEE YOU AGAIN, LUCILLE! DON'T TELL ME YOU'VE GOT NEW PROTOTYPES ALREADY!

I'M WEARING THEM RIGHT NOW. WANNA SEE?

LUCE, THOSE ARE DOWNRIGHT ELEGANT.

I KNOW! MY MANUFACTURERS KNOW HOW TO MAKE ME HAPPY.

I WISH I COULD SHOW YOU HOW THESE NEW MODELS CONNECT TO THE BODY, BUT I CAN'T HIKE MY SKIRT THAT FAR UP –

BRENDAN.

IF YOU'RE FINISHED, WE SHOULD GET OUR STUFF BACKSTAGE.

GO AHEAD, AL.

I GOTTA TALK TO MAGGIE ONCE SHE'S DONE WITH HER PRESENTATION, AND THAT SHOULD BE IN JUST A MINUTE.

FINE. SEE YOU IN THE BACK.

JUST AS CHARMING AS EVER, I SEE.

HA HA. YUP.

– AND USING THIS *MAGNETIC PLATFORM*, I'VE CREATED A SCULPTURE THAT WILL CONSTANTLY CHANGE SHAPE –

WITHOUT REPETITION –

FOREVER.

SHNK

SHNK SHNK

THANK YOU.

CLAP CLHP CLA

CLAP CLAP

LAP CLAP

CLAP

SHNK SHNK SHNK

SHNK SHNK

GREE ROOM → STAGI

LIVE

BRENDAN, I *GOTTA* ASK.

HOW CAN YOU *WORK* WITH A GUY LIKE THAT?

WHAT DO YOU MEAN?

WELL, YOU KNOW, HE SEEMS SO . . .

RESERVED?

ALOOF. INTIMIDATING.

I KNOW YOU'RE STILL STARTING OUT, SWEETIE BUT YOU DON'T HAVE TO PU UP WITH ANY *NONSENSE* THA MAN GIVES YOU. YOUR CAREE DESERVES *BETTER* THAN THA

I APPRECIATE THE THOUGHT, LUCE. I DO.

BUT I *LIKE* WORKING WITH AL. HE JUST... HASN'T REALIZED THAT GETTING ALONG WITH OTHERS CAN HELP GET HIS IDEAS OFF THE GROUND. I CAN *FIX* THAT.

BRENDAN!

MAGGIE, HEY!

I TOLD THEM TO LEAVE EVERYTHING ON THE STAGE. YOU SHOULD BE ABLE TO CONNECT YOUR COMPUTERS WITH NO TROUBLE.

GREAT. PERFECT. I CAN'T THANK YOU *ENOUGH,* MAGGIE. YOUR EQUIPMENT IS GONNA MAKE OUR DEMO *UNFORGETTABLE.*

YOU BOYS BREAK A LEG.

WHAT WAS *THAT* ALL ABOUT?

YOU'LL SEE.

YOU'RE ADORABLE. YOU SURE YOU WON'T CONSIDER A CAREER IN PROSTHETICS?

I'M MORE INTERESTED IN ROBOTIC *BRAINS* THAN I AM IN *LIMBS,* LUCE.

AND I'M SURE YOU'LL GO FAR.

JUST DON'T LET ANYONE HOLD YOU BACK, BRENDAN.

...AND ONCE I REALIZED I'D BROKEN IT, I DECIDED I HAD TO *REPLACE* IT WITHOUT BRENDAN FINDING OUT.

SO WHILE HE WAS AT WORK I SPENT THE WHOLE DAY MAKING A NEW COMPONENT FROM *SCRATCH*.

YOU DID *NOT.*

I TOTALLY DID! IT WAS SO DUMB. I DIDN'T REALIZE HOW COMMON THE PART WAS.

I COULD HAVE BOUGHT ONE DOWN AT THE *HARDWARE STORE.*

HA HA HA HA

SOUNDS LIKE YOU'RE FEELING BETTER.

I AM.

I AM, THANK YOU.

LISTEN, KID. IT'S NICE OF YOU TO GET ME OUT OF THE HOUSE AND EVERYTHING –

BUT I DON'T WAN[T] TO *CRAMP YOUR STYLE* YOU CAN LET ME EXPLOR[E] ON MY OWN FOR A WHILE GO HANG OUT WITH YOU[R] *FRIENDS* OR WHATEVE[R] IT IS YOU USUALLY D[O]

OH! NO, THAT'S OKAY. I'M USUALLY ON MY OWN MOST OF THE TIME, ANYWAY. I LIKE HAVING SOMEONE TO WALK AROUND WITH.

YOU NEVER HANG OUT WITH OTHER KIDS?

I, UM. NO?

I MEAN, HIGH SCHOOLERS ALREADY *KNOW* EACH OTHER.

FROM SCHOOL AND STUFF.

THEY WOULDN'T KNOW ME.

PLUS, I CAN'T TALK TO PEOPLE THE WAY *BRENDAN* CAN. I JUST . . . GET *NERVOUS* AND *WEIRD* SOMETIMES.

WEIRD? MAYBE. BUT *NERVOUS* I FIND HARD TO BELIEVE.

WELL, OKAY, SEE THOSE GIRLS OVER THERE?

I COULDN'T JUST GO OVER THERE AND —

WHERE'RE YOU GOING?

FORGOT SOMETHING.

THE LIBRARY. WE GOTTA GO BACK TO THE LIBRARY.

WE WENT. AND ISN'T THIS THE BUS WE WANT?

I GOTTA GET A BOOK AT THE LIBRARY.

IT'S JUST A TEN MINUTES' WALK BACK.

FIND ANOTHER BOOK TO ADD TO THE PILE?

YUP. NOW I JUST GOTTA TRACK DOWN ONE MORE MECHANICAL DIAGRAM AND –

YOU COULD TRY ASKING YOUR **STUDY BUDDIES** OVER THERE FOR HELP.

. . . YEAH. I JUST – YOU WERE RIGHT. I **DON'T** KNOW A LOT OF OTHER KIDS.

BECAUSE YOU FOLLOW THEM AROUND LIKE A WEIRDO.

SSSH!

I USED TO DO THE SAME THING, WHEN I DIDN'T KNOW ANY BETTER.

. . . YOU DID?

YEAH. I DID.

THE HUMAN BRAIN EXCELS AT **SOCIALIZING**. IT DEVELOPED OVER MILLIONS OF YEARS TO DO PRECISELY THAT.

BUT AS ADAPTABLE AND EFFICIENT AS THE BRAIN IS, IT CAN STILL MISJUDGE SITUATIONS AND MAKE MISTAKES.

AND THOSE MISTAKES CAN **HURT**.

WHEN I WAS YOUNGER, I WAS AFRAID OF MAKING THOSE MISTAKES. SO FOR A WHILE, I JUST. . . DIDN'T BOTHER TO INTERACT WITH OTHER PEOPLE.

BUT THAT'S NOT WHAT BRAINS ARE **FOR**. EVENTUALLY, I FIGURED OUT HOW TO DEAL WITH OTHER PEOPLE AND BE **SMART** ABOUT IT.

IT TAKES PRACTICE, BUT YOU'LL LEARN. JUST LIKE I DID.

I GUESS, BUT... I DIDN'T MEAN TO BE *WEIRD* ABOUT IT.

I ALWAYS SEE A LOT OF KIDS FROM THE HIGH SCHOOL A FEW BLOCKS SOUTH OF HERE. BUT WHEN I SAW THOSE GIRLS AT THE BUS STOP, I JUST ...

DO YOU EVER JUST *NOTICE* SOMEONE? AND THINK, MAYBE — MAYBE THAT PERSON'S LIKE *ME.*

I MEAN, LIKE, MAYBE I WOULD HAVE ...

SOMETHING IN *COMMON* WITH THEM.

AND MAYBE WE WOULD GET ALON—

IS IT THE GIRL WITH THE EARPIECE?

NO!

WAIT, WHY?

IT'S ATTACHED TO HER HEAD. WITH *WIRES.*

SO? LOTS OF PEOPLE HAVE THOSE.

YOU MEAN IT'S NOT BECAUSE SHE'S ANOTHER RO –

NOT HERE.

THIS ISN'T LIKE LEM'S WHERE EVERYBODY KNOWS. THERE ARE PEOPLE HERE.

IF I'M NOT AT LEM'S OR HIDING SOMEWHERE DEEP IN THE PARK GETTING READY TO FLY HOME, I'M AROUND PEOPLE.

AND IF I DON'T STAND OUT, I GET TO WALK AROUND PEOPLE LIKE I'M ONE OF THEM.

I DON'T WANT PEOPLE TO LOOK TWICE. I DON'T WANT PEOPLE TO ASK.

PEOPLE LIKE TO KNOW WHAT YOU ARE. IF YOU CONFUSE THEM THEN THE QUESTIONS START.

MOST OF THEM AREN'T EVEN TRYING TO BE MEAN WHEN THEY ASK.

BUT I DON'T WANT THEM TO ASK.

THEY WON'T.

YOU'VE DONE ENOUGH FOR ME TODAY. I'LL TELL YOU WHAT.

I'LL GO BACK TO STERLING TO MEET BRENDAN, YOU CATCH UP WITH US LATER.

I GOTTA GO IN THROUGH THE BACK ENTRANCE, RIGHT?

YEAH, BUT –

YOU WANT TO BE AROUND PEOPLE, RIGHT? YOU'RE A SMART KID. JUST ACT SMART.

DO WHATEVER IT TAKES IN ORDER TO PASS.

AND THEY WON'T ASK.

OKAY.

IF YOU DON'T THINK THEY'LL SUSPECT . . .

FOR SOME REASON, WHEN YOU SAY IT, I BELIEVE IT.

THANK YOU, MR. STERLING. FOR EVERYTHING.

I KNEW YOU'D KNOW WHAT TO DO. MAYBE THIS WILL WORK.

I CAN DO THIS!

I CAN'T DO THIS.

WHAT WERE WE *THINKING?!*

WHAT MADE US THINK WE WERE EVEN *REMOTELY* READY TO DO THE DEMO IN FRONT OF HUNDREDS OF PEOPLE?

AND WE'RE GOING UP AFTER *LUCILLE!*

AN A.I. CON VETERAN WITH THE SEXIEST PROTOTYPE I'VE EVER SEEN!

I COULD HEAR HER APPLAUSE FROM HERE! I COULD HEAR IT FROM THE *BATHROOM.*

STAGE

QUIET PLEASE

I'M GOING TO PUKE.

I'M GOING TO PUKE ON THE EMULATOR AND THEN I AM GOING TO *DIE.*

YOU THINK YOU CAN DIAL IT DOWN OVER THERE WHILE I FINISH THIS DIAGNOSTIC?

OH, I'M SORRY, AM I NOT PLAYING IT *COOL* ENOUGH FOR YOU RIGHT NOW?

I'M *SAYING* THAT WE'RE GOING UP THERE IN FIVE MINUTES AND THAT WE SHOULD BE AS READY AS WE *CAN* BE.

THAT DOESN'T MEAN I'M NOT ALLOWED TO BE *NERVOUS* —

AND WHAT ABOUT *ME*? YOU THINK I'M NOT?

I'LL DO MY PART. I'LL BE THERE WITH YOU.

BUT THE DEMO WASN'T *MY* IDEA. I JUST WANT TO GET BACK TO WORK.

GREEN ROOM

149

LADIES AND GENTLEMEN, THIS IS THE **STERLING NEURON EMULATOR**. A PROCESSOR DESIGNED TO READ, TRANSLATE, AND **EMULATE** THE SPECIFIC PATTERNS OF AN INDIVIDUAL BRAIN.

NOW, PROJECTS TO MODEL AN ENTIRE HUMAN BRAIN ARE ALREADY UNDERWAY. NEEDLESS TO SAY, THEY HAVE MORE **RESOURCES** AND **MANPOWER** THAN WE DO.

BUT STERLING IS DEVELOPING A **COMPACT, ADAPTABLE** DEVICE THAT WILL EMULATE A **SPECIFIC** BRAIN, WITH THE HIGHEST FIDELITY POSSIBLE.

AND WE CAN DO THAT THANKS TO THE **NEURONS** AL DESIGNED FOR US. UNLIKE EARLIER SYNTHETIC MODELS, THESE NEURONS AREN'T LIMITED TO FUNCTIONING IN **BINARY**. THEY'RE FASTER AND FAR MORE FLEXIBLE.

AL'S MADE OUR JOB **MUCH** EASIER.

BUT IF YOU REALLY WANT TO SEE *HOW* MUCH EASIER, I THINK A PRACTICAL DEMONSTRATION IS IN ORDER!

NOW FOR THIS, I'M GOING TO EED A GORGEOUS OLUNTEER FROM THE AUDIENCE —

YOU, SIR! HOW ABOUT IT?

HA HA HA HA HA HA

NO? WELL, YOUR *FRIEND* THERE WILL DO JUST AS WELL. COME ON UP.

HA HA HA

WHAT'S YOUR NAME, MISS?

HELENA.

THANK YOU FOR YOUR HELP, HELENA. PLEASE TAKE A SEAT.

AL, THE *TIARA*, PLEASE.

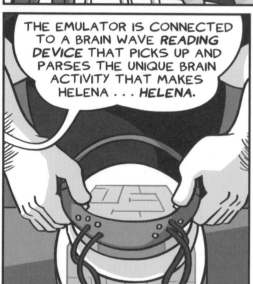

THE EMULATOR IS CONNECTED TO A BRAIN WAVE *READING DEVICE* THAT PICKS UP AND PARSES THE UNIQUE BRAIN ACTIVITY THAT MAKES HELENA . . . *HELENA.*

THE LONGER SHE WEARS IT, THE MORE COMPLEX THE COPY GENERATED BY THE EMULATOR.

FOR OUR PURPOSES TODAY, 60 SECONDS WILL SUFFICE.

BUT WE'LL GIVE HER SOMETHING TO *THINK ABOUT* FOR THOSE 60 SECONDS.

HELENA, PLEASE OPEN THIS LAPTOP AND PRESS THE SPACE BAR WHEN YOU'RE READY.

WHAT HELENA'S LOOKING AT IS A LITTLE *BRAIN-TEASER.*

AS SHE'S FIGURING OUT A WAY TO SOLVE IT, THE READING DEVICE IS TRANSFERRING THOSE UNIQUE NEURAL IMPULSES TO OUR *PROXY ROBOT* IN THE CASE OVER THERE.

THE PROXY IS STILL IN DEVELOPMENT, BUT WE COULDN'T RESIST INCLUDING IT IN OUR DEMO.

AFTER ALL, IT'S AWFULLY *CUTE.*

YOUR MINUTE'S UP, HELENA. CLOSE THE LAPTOP. I'LL TAKE BOTH OF THOSE BACK.

DO YOU MIND STAYING UP HERE FOR A LITTLE WHILE LONGER?

AL, PLEASE ACTIVATE HELENA'S PROXY.

KLIK

VRR

KCHAK

AL, PLEASE ACTIVATE THE PLATFORM.

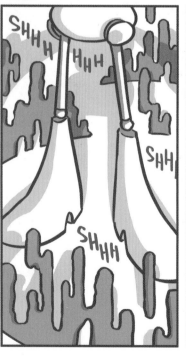

SHHHH
HHH
SHH
SHHH

SHNK
SHNK
SHNK
SHNK
SHNK

THE IMAGE WE GAVE HELENA A CHANCE TO LOOK AT WAS A *MAZE.*

IT WAS RANDOMLY GENERATED USING **MS. MAGNUSSON'S** ALGORITHMS, AND HER MAGNETIC PLATFORM RENDERS IT IN 3D.

NOBODY HERE HAS SEEN THIS MAZE OR HAD THE TIME TO EXAMINE IT EXCEPT FOR *HELENA* . . .

VRRR

. . . AND HER *PROXY.*

AND IT LOOKS LIKE HER PROXY HAS AN IDEA OF HOW TO GET OUT!

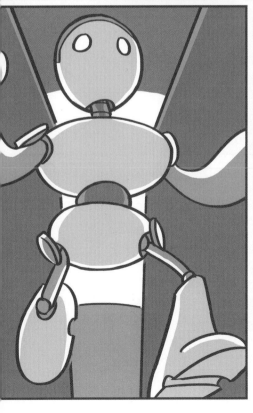

WAIT!

THERE'S ONE MORE TRICK I'D LIKE TO TRY.

HELENA. FIND A FRIEND.

WHO'S THAT YOUNG LADY YOUR PROXY'S FOUND OVER THERE?

WELL, I DON'T KNOW HOW IT –

BUT THAT'S –

– MY GIRLFRIEND.

LADIES AND GENTLEMEN, PLEASE GIVE HELENA A BIG ROUND OF APPLAUSE!

THAT *LAST* BIT ISN'T PART OF THE OFFICIAL EXPERIMENT BY ANY MEANS.

BUT WHEN WE STARTED DOING TRIAL RUNS, AL NOTICED THAT A FEW EXTRA *SNAPSHOTS* WOULD SLIP INTO THE DATA.

VRRRRₖ

YOUR PROXY MIGHT RUN OUT OF THE MAZE AND PERFORM A DANCE ROUTINE YOU LEARNED WHEN YOU WERE **SIX**. IT MIGHT RECOGNIZE THE FACE OF A FRIEND, OR A *LOVED ONE*.

RRRRₖ KLIK

THE SNAPSHOTS ARE ALWAYS . . . A *SURPRISE*.

159

BUT THEY DON'T HAVE TO BE.

IT IS WITHIN OUR POWER TO CAPTURE MORE THAN A *GLIMPSE* OF A PERSON'S THOUGHTS.

WITH THE RIGHT TOOLS, IT WILL SOON BE POSSIBLE TO TRANSFER, EVEN *DUPLICATE* AN ENTIRE MIND –

– A HUMAN IDENTITY.

THINK OF THE *PRACTICAL* APPLICATIONS OF SUCH TECHNOLOGY.

WE CAN OBSERVE AND STUDY OUR OWN BRAINS, AND USE THAT KNOWLEDGE TO TREAT *ILLNESS* AND NURTURE *GENIUS.*

WE CAN ARCHIVE BRILLIANT MINDS AS EFFORTLESSLY AS WE PRESERVE *BOOKS.*

WE WOULDN'T HAVE TO RELAY INSTRUCTIONS TO ROBOTS EXPLORING THE DEPTHS OF THE *OCEAN* OR THE VASTNESS OF *SPACE* . . .

WE CAN UPLOAD OUR MINDS INTO THOSE ROBOTS AND GO THERE OURSELVES.

WE CAN OFFER THE *SICK* AND DYING A WAY TO *FREE THEMSELVES* FROM AN ABBREVIATED LIFE OF PAIN –

WE CAN OFFER THEM NEW VESSELS TO *HOUSE THEIR SOULS.*

ALL OF THAT IS AHEAD OF US. WE CAN TAKE YOU THERE.

. . . WITH THE HELP OF SOME GENEROUS INVESTORS, OF COURSE. RIGHT, AL?

HA HA HA HA HA HA

YEAH.

HA HA HA

HA HA HA

WELL, THAT'S ALL I'M GETTING OUT OF HIM FOR NOW!

BUT WE'LL BOTH BE AVAILABLE TO ANSWER QUESTIONS ON THE CONFERENCE FLOOR. THAT'S BEEN OUR DEMONSTRATION!

THANK YOU SO MUCH!

CLAP CLAP CLAP CLAP CLAP CLAP WHOOO

FOLLOW ME.

ALL RIGHT, AL, I GET IT. I WAS TOO OVER THE TOP.

YOU DON'T HAVE TO TELL ME HOW BADLY I FFFMMMF—

MMMMMMMMMMM

STAGE

YOU WERE AMAZING.

DID YOU AD-LIB THAT ENTIRE SECOND HALF?

. . . I DUNNO. I DON'T REMEMBER. I THINK I *BLACKED OUT* AS SOON AS I STARTED TALKING.

I'LL HAVE TO WATCH THE VIDEO OF IT LATER –

YOU CONVINCED THEM THAT WE WERE DOING SOMETHING *IMPORTANT.*

AND THAT I HAD A *PART* IN IT. IT FELT LIKE I WAS ACTUALLY *THERE.*

YOU *WERE* THERE, YOU WEIRDO. YOU DID GREAT, TOO. EVERYONE *LIKED* YOU.

D'YOU THINK YOU CAN MUSTER MORE THAN ONE SYLLABLE FOR ALL OF THE BRAND NEW CUSTOMERS WHO'LL WANT TO ASK US QUESTIONS?

YEAH, OF COURSE. IT'S DIFFERENT WHEN YOU'RE NOT ON A *STAGE.*

I KNOW.

THIS IS YOUR TIME TO SHINE, TOO, AL. AND YOU *WILL.*

JUST KEEP GOING.

EXCUSE ME –

I NEED TO LOOK FOR ONE MORE BOOK BUT I'VE GOT TOO MANY ON MY HANDS AS IT IS IS IT OKAY IF I SET 'EM DOWN FOR A SECOND I MEAN JUST FOR A SECOND –

OKAY THANKS I'LL BE RIGHT BACK JUST GOTTA GO FIND THAT BOOK NOW –

HERE YOU GO.

I'M SORRY. I PEEKED AT THE BOOK ON TOP OF THE STACK.

COLLOIDAL CONDUCTORS

WHAT'S A COLLOIDAL CONDUCTOR?

IT'S, UM.

A DEVICE USED TO DIRECT THE DISTRIBUTION OF NANOSCOPIC MACHINES ACROSS A SURFACE WITH AN ELECTRIC CHARGE.

THEY'RE USED A LOT IN PROSTHETICS AND SYNTHETIC DESIGN.

NANO-LIKE NANO-BOTS?

ARE YOU A ROBOTICS PERSON?

I.

I MEAN, ARE YOU GETTING YOUR DEGREE IN ROBOTICS? YOU STUDY AT THE U, DON'T YOU?

NO! OH, NO. I'M ONLY 15.

OH! ME, TOO. OKAY. YOU JUST SEEMED REALLY . . .

. . . GROWN UP.

OH MY *GOD*, TY.

OF ALL THE WAYS TO SHIRK GROUP WORK, YOU PICKED THE *BEST* WAY.

I'M SO SORRY! I DIDN'T MEAN TO *DISTRACT* YOU –

AW, NO SWEAT.

TY'S GOT A BIT OF A TALENT FOR CHATTING UP *OLDER GIRLS.*

SHE'S *OUR AGE!* AND I WANTED TO KNOW WHAT SHE WAS READING!

UH HUH.

I – I THOUGHT MAYBE HER BOOKS COULD HELP WITH OUR *ASSIGNMENT.* SHE WAS TALKING ABOUT *NANOBOTS* AND MAYBE WE COULD *WRITE* ABOUT THEM –

WAIT, YOU GUYS ARE WORKING ON A SCIENCE PROJECT?

BECAUSE I WAS TELLING HER – HIM – YOUR *FRIEND* – ABOUT COLLOIDAL CONDUCTORS –

YOU CAN MAKE A COLLOID – A *FLUID* – THAT CONTAINS THOUSANDS OF NANOSCOPIC MACHINES, RIGHT?

IF YOU ARRANGE A FEW CONDUCTORS OVER THE SURFACE OF AN OBJECT, THE ELECTRIC CHARGE WILL *FLATTEN* THE FLUID INTO A SMOOTH FLEXIBLE LAYER OVER THE TOP.

THEN THE NANO-MACHINES CAN RECORD DATA LIKE PRESSURE AND TEMPERATURE AND *PROTECT* WHATEVER'S UNDERNEATH.

THERE'S A PROSTHETIC LIMB COMPANY THAT PATENTED A FLUID THAT THEY USE AS A KIND OF *SKIN.* IT'S SUPER . . .

. . . COOL.

I'M SULLA.

WELL, HOW 'BOUT THAT.

SULLA, HUH? I'M **NEESHA.** THAT'S RUQIYO, AND ERIKA. YOU'VE MET **TY.**

YOU A GRADE ABOVE US? HOW COME WE HAVEN'T SEEN YOU AROUND?

WELL, YOU WOULDN'T HAVE. I'M HOME-SCHOOLED.

NO KIDDING? SO YOUR **MOM'S** GIVING YOU ALL OF THIS READING?

IT'S MY **DAD,** BUT YEAH.

D'YOU KNOW AS MUCH ABOUT ORGANIC CHEMISTRY AS YOU DO ABOUT NANO-BOTS? LIKE, OSMOSIS?

AND MITO-CHONDRIA?

AND WRITING A PAPER ON CELLULAR STRUCTURE IN A GROUP OF FOUR TO FIVE PEOPLE?

WOULDN'T SAY **THAT,** UT . . . DO YOU WANT ME TO ELP YOU FIND SOME BOOKS?

WOULD YOU? AW MAN, THAT WOULD BE SUPER HELPFUL. MR. GILMORE'S MAKING US CITE BOOKS. **PAPER BOOKS.**

WHY DON'T YOU GO WITH HER, TY? START PULLING YOUR WEIGHT AROUND HERE.

KAY. WE WON'T BE LONG, IT SOUNDS LIKE YOU GUYS ARE REAL BUSY –

H, DON'T WORRY!

TAKE YOUR TI-I-I-I-IME!

YOU GUYS ARE **MEAN.**

PLEASE. THOSE TWO NEEDED ANOTHER TEN MINUTES TO FIGURE OUT EACH OTHER'S GEEK FREQUENCY. I AM THE **BEST** FRIEND.

THANKS FOR PUTTING UP WITH THIS. YOU REALLY *ARE* BEING HELPFUL. IT TAKES SO LONG TO GO THROUGH ALL OF THESE BOOKS TRYING TO FIND THE BEST ONE.

AW, I *LIKE* THAT, THOUGH. YOU ALWAYS FIND SOMETHING REALLY COOL NEXT TO THE BOOK YOU WERE ACTUALLY LOOKING FOR.

YEAH.

CAN I ASK YOU A QUESTION?

SURE!

ARE YOU NAMED AFTER THE GENERAL?

. . . HUH?

LUCIUS CORNELIUS SULLA. HE WAS A GENERAL. IN ANCIENT ROME.

OH NO, IT'S A GIRL'S NAME, TOO. I SAW –

MY *DAD* SAW IT IN A BOOK HE LIKED.

YOU LIKE HISTORY?

MY DAD TEACHES IT. AND I KNOW MORE ABOUT IT THAN NANOBOTS AND SYNTHETIC STUFF.

IS THAT WHAT YOUR DAD DOES? IS THAT WHY *YOU* STUDY IT?

YEAH, BUT EVEN IF HE DIDN'T –

HE LETS ME STUDY ANYTHING I LIKE. AND I *REALLY* LIKE THIS.

IT'S NICE TO KNOW THAT HE'S OKAY WITH WHAT- EVER I DO.

THAT'S COOL. HE LOOKED PRETTY **STRICT**.

WHAT?

THAT GUY WITH THE GRAY HAIR WHO WAS HERE WITH YOU. HE'S YOUR DAD, ISN'T HE?

YYYYYYYEEEAH. THAT'S HIM.

HE'S NOT HERE ANYMORE, HE HAD TO—

GO RUN ERRANDS. **LOTS** OF ERRANDS.

HEY, THIS BOOK IS A GOOD START! LET'S SHOW THE OTHERS WHAT WE FOUND.

I DIDN'T MEAN TO MAKE YOU STICK AROUND AS LONG AS YOU DID.

BUT IF YOU AREN'T BUSY, SULLA . . .

WOULD YOU LIKE TO . . .

. . . STUDY WITH US FOR A WHILE?

OKAY, TY.

I DON'T CARE HOW SMART SHE IS, TY, SHE'S **NOT** WRITING YOUR PART OF THE OUTLINE FOR YOU!

ERIKA, OH MY GOD, THIS IS A **LIBRARY**!

I, UH. THINK I'VE GOT AN APPOINTMENT WITH YOUR BOSS.

THIS IS THE BACK ENTRANCE, RIGHT?

YEAH, I GET IT. ALL RIGHT. THAT'S JUST WHAT I LOOK LIKE.

CAN I GO UP NOW?

DING

OH, HEY! GOOD TIMING!

COME ON IN, YOU TWO, I'M JUST TIDYING UP A BIT -

OH.

. . . WHERE'S SULLA?

STILL AT THE LIBRARY.

SHE HAD SOMETHING TO DO, SO I TOLD HER I'D BE FINE ON MY OWN. SHE GOT THESE FOR YOU.

OH! SHE DIDN'T HAVE TO -

WELL, MAYBE IT'S FOR THE BEST THAT SHE ISN'T HERE. WE MIGHT COVER A LITTLE MORE GROUND WITHOUT HER HOVERING AROUND THE DIAGNOSTIC PLATFORM.

THIS TABLE? WHAT ARE WE GONNA BE LOOKING AT?

WELL, HERE'S THE THING . . .

I HAVE TO . . . POKE AROUND A LITTLE BIT.

INSIDE ME.

I'LL JUST RUN A SCAN - IT'LL BE QUICK AND NONINVASIVE. BUT LISTEN, THIS WHOLE MYSTERY HAS TURNED INTO A SECURITY ISSUE.

SOMEONE'S GONE THROUGH MY PERSONAL PROPERTY WITHOUT MY KNOWLEDGE. YOUR . . . MAKERS MAY HAVE ILLEGALLY ACCESSED STERLING TECHNOLOGY, AND IF YOUR NEW BODY CAN OFFER UP ANY CLUES -

OKAY.

O - OKAY?

OKAY, ALL RIGHT. I AGREE. LET'S DO THIS.

SULLA DOESN'T KNOW.

ABOUT US? OF COURSE SHE DOESN'T KNOW.

WHEN YOU SAID YOU NEVER TOLD *ANYBODY* — I GUESS I DIDN'T FIGURE YOU'D KEEP IT A SECRET FROM *HER*.

WHAT, YOU THOUGHT I'D TELL HER, "SWEETIE, YOU KNOW THAT GUY WHOSE MIND AND PERSONALITY IS THE ENTIRE BASIS FOR YOUR EXISTENCE? YEAH, ABOUT HIM . . ."

I'M TRYING TO RAISE A *WELL-ADJUSTED* MEMBER OF SOCIETY AND I DON'T THINK TELLING HER *THAT* WOULD HAVE HELPED.

YOU . . . REALLY THINK OF HER AS YOUR *KID*, DON'T YOU?

YES.

YES, I DO.

BRENDAN, I'M SORRY.

I SHOULD HAVE LISTENED TO YOU FROM THE START.

YOU HAD EVERY REASON NOT TO. IT'S OKAY.

HERE'S YOUR SHIRT. I'M ALL DONE.

I'LL SCRUB THIS COMPUTER AND BRING THE DATA HOME WITH ME. IT'LL TAKE A WHILE TO PROPERLY ANALYZE, BUT WHAT I'M SEEING HERE SEEMS REALLY STRANGE.

HOW'S THAT?

WELL, SUPERFICIALLY, YOUR DESIGN LOOKS LIKE HEAVILY MODIFIED STERLING WORK, RIGHT?

BUT IN A LOT OF WAYS YOUR WIRING LOOKS LIKE HOW I USED TO DO THINGS PRE-STERLING. HOW WE USED TO DO THINGS.

ONE THING'S FOR SURE, THIS COPYCAT WAS THOROUGH. THEY DIDN'T MISS A SINGLE . . .

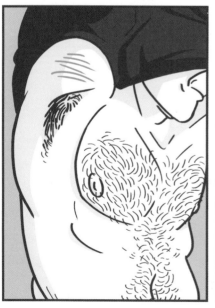

. . . DETAIL.

IS THIS SULLA?

WHAT?

IN THIS PICTURE. IS THIS WHAT SHE LOOKED LIKE BEFORE SHE —

— BEFORE YOU CHANGED HER?

AL, THAT'S *YOU.*

SULLA ASKED ME TO PUT AWAY HER OLDER PHOTOS. THEY'RE IN THE HOUSE SOMEWHERE. I *FOUND* THIS ONE.

SKRITCH SKRITCH

THAT'S MY RADIO KIT. I REMEMBER THAT NOW. BUT I DON'T THINK I'VE EVEN SEEN THIS PICTURE BEFORE.

I HADN'T SEEN IT, EITHER. A MAGAZINE DUG IT UP TO USE IN SOME *IN MEMORIAM* THING THEY DID FOR YOU, NOT LONG AFTER YOU . . .

. . . ANYWAY, I NORMALLY DON'T PAY ATTENTION TO THOSE THINGS, BUT.

I LIKED THIS LITTLE KID.

177

HOW DID I DIE?

THEY SAID IT WAS CALLED GOODPASTURE'S SYNDROME. IT'S AN AUTOIMMUNE DISEASE.

YOU'D HAD AN INFECTION – MAYBE FOR *YEARS* – AND THE EARLY SYMPTOMS WERE *LITTLE* THINGS LIKE FATIGUE AND SHORTNESS OF BREATH.

BUT THEN YOU *OVEREXERTED* YOURSELF . . .

YOUR ANTIBODIES ATTACKED YOUR LUNGS AND KIDNEYS, THEY SAID, AND YOU DIDN'T REALIZE HOW BAD IT WAS UNTIL YOU STARTED COUGHING UP BLOOD.

YOUR BODY WAS REJECTING ITS OWN ORGANS.

WHEN I SAW THEM PUTTING YOU IN THE AMBULANCE, I –

HEH.

I THOUGHT *YOU'D* DONE ALL THAT –

TO YOURSELF.

I WAS OUT OF MY *MIND*, OF COURSE. BUT I FOLLOWED YOU TO THE HOSPITAL AND TOOK THE NEURON EMULATOR WITH ME.

IN THE END, I HAD *HER*. I HAD SULL.

BUT I STILL . . .

I STILL MISSED YOU SO MUCH.

I'M SORRY.

I DON'T HAVE ANY ANSWERS FOR YOU. I DON'T KNOW HOW YOU GOT HERE.

HOW DID I DO THIS, ALL THOSE YEARS AGO? HOW WAS I SO SURE OF EVERYTHING?

YOU'RE A DIFFERENT PERSON NOW.

YOU'RE A GOOD FATHER.

AL, I —

...IT'S SULLA. SHE WANTS US TO PICK HER UP AT THE LIBRARY.

LET'S HAVE GIMEL BRING THE CAR AROUND TO THE BACK.

library. when you and mr sterling are done can you pick me up?

- PICK UP SULLA (just added)

- 4:00 CST Return home

- 4:30 CST Load DRIVE A, sweep sequence

- FRIDAY Contact member new list: POSSIBLE

ct members o st: POSSIBLE S

HEY, KID.

HI, MR. STERLING.

WHO WERE THOSE GIRLS YOU WERE TALKING TO?

OH! . . . NOBODY, REALLY. JUST SOME HIGH SCHOOL KIDS WORKING ON A PROJECT.

AND HOW'S YOUR PROJECT GOING?

I - I'VE GOT A GOOD START. THANK YOU FOR YOUR ADVICE EARLIER.

I KNEW YOU'D BE FINE. YOU'RE A SMART GIRL.

I'M GLAD I'M NOT THE ONLY ONE. THOSE GIRLS WERE REALLY COOL. I'M GLAD I WAS ABLE TO . . .

. . . HELP.

You can call me Titus.

t.trang@ 612.30'47.3

WELL, IT'S GOOD THAT YOU AND AL GOT A DAY TO YOURSELVES.

LET'S GO MAKE SOME DINNER AND YOU CAN TELL ME ALL ABOUT IT.

"IN ATTEMPTING TO CONSTRUCT SUCH MACHINES
WE SHOULD NOT BE IRREVERENTLY USURPING
[GOD'S] POWER OF CREATING SOULS, ANY MORE
THAN WE ARE IN THE PROCREATION OF CHILDREN:
RATHER WE ARE, IN EITHER CASE,
INSTRUMENTS OF HIS WILL PROVIDING
MANSIONS FOR THE SOULS THAT HE CREATES."

- A.M. TURING,
COMPUTING MACHINERY AND INTELLIGENCE
1950

DREAM 8/31   (BACK to WEIRD DREAMS, woo!)

So I had to stop and think about this one a bit
before writing to make it a little more coherent.
I guess a man who had been famous for something
(like a scientist, or a theorist, I remember video
game developer?), anyway, someone brilliant had
died, but then a copy of his brain was found on
file in some forgotten place. They bring him back
to life in a body resembling his original one,
and when he asks why, they say it was part of
a stipulation he made to his scientific partner and
best friend. He goes to visit this friend, who look
older than him by this point, and learns that he
had himself been working with an incomplete version
of the man's brain, raising it as a new person, in order
to preserve his unique genius. This person is a human
robot with superpowers — kind of like Astro Boy, really
but the robot resembles a 15-year old girl. Her "fath
sheepishly explains that the gender switch was her prefe
From here the plot gets fuzzier, but I remember the

I think this could actually be a super-interesting story
if it focuses on the relationship between the two scientist
and the man's own hidden feelings.

The revived man. (Maybe he dresses kind of like Steve Jobs?)

His friend (kind of hairless, with overbite)

the girl (similar facial structure to the revived man)

Sketches from 8/31 dream (see following page)

THE FIRST SKETCHES OF THE CHARACTERS THAT WOULD BECOME AL, BRENDAN, AND SULLA.

BLAH BLAH BLAH

PTCHOOOOO

BRENDAN

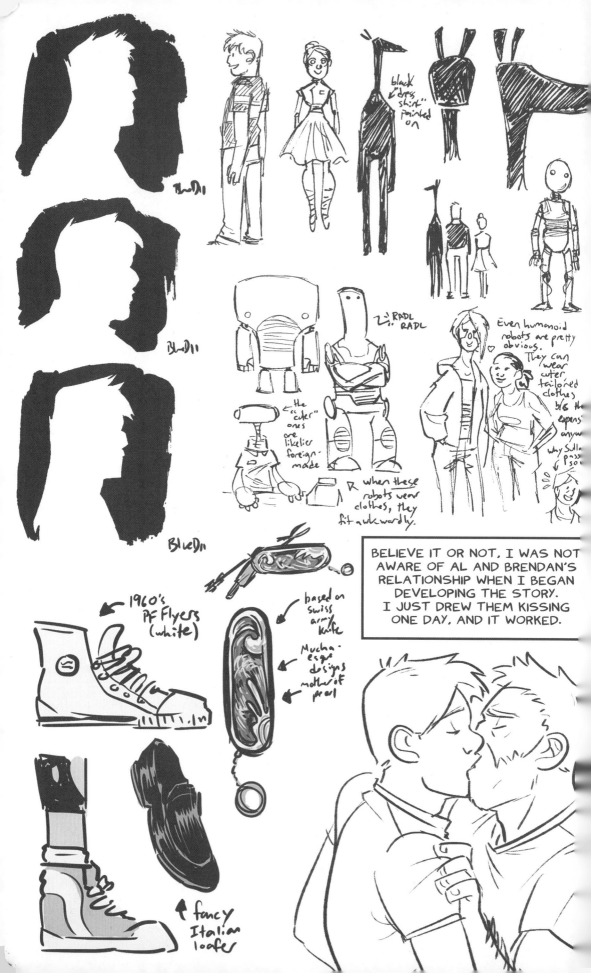

BluD11

BluD11

BlueD11

black "dress" shirt painted on

2" RADL
RADL

Even humanoid robots are pretty obvious. They can wear cuter tailored clothes b/c the expens... anyw...

Why Sulla... pass... som...

the "cuter" ones are likelier foreign-made

R when these robots wear clothes, they fit awkwardly.

based on swiss army knife

Mucha-esque designs mother of pearl

1960's PF Flyers (white)

fancy Italian loafer

BELIEVE IT OR NOT, I WAS NOT AWARE OF AL AND BRENDAN'S RELATIONSHIP WHEN I BEGAN DEVELOPING THE STORY. I JUST DREW THEM KISSING ONE DAY, AND IT WORKED.

UCILLE VILLAS SANTOS
2002   age 28   —A
                  —S
                  —B

shaggy hair

high collars

scarf

faint brows

cuffs

—S

—T

T.T. prelim. designs

BwDz

PRELIMINARY DESIGNS
FOR LUCILLE, TITUS,
AND THE TEENS.

TITUS TRANG
2021   age 15

bashful
quiet
thought-ful

NEESHA
2021   age 15

-energetic
-up-front
-demanding

RUQIYO
2021 age 16

-bright
- good right-hand man

ERIKA
2021   age 15

-snarky
-deadpan
- nerdy

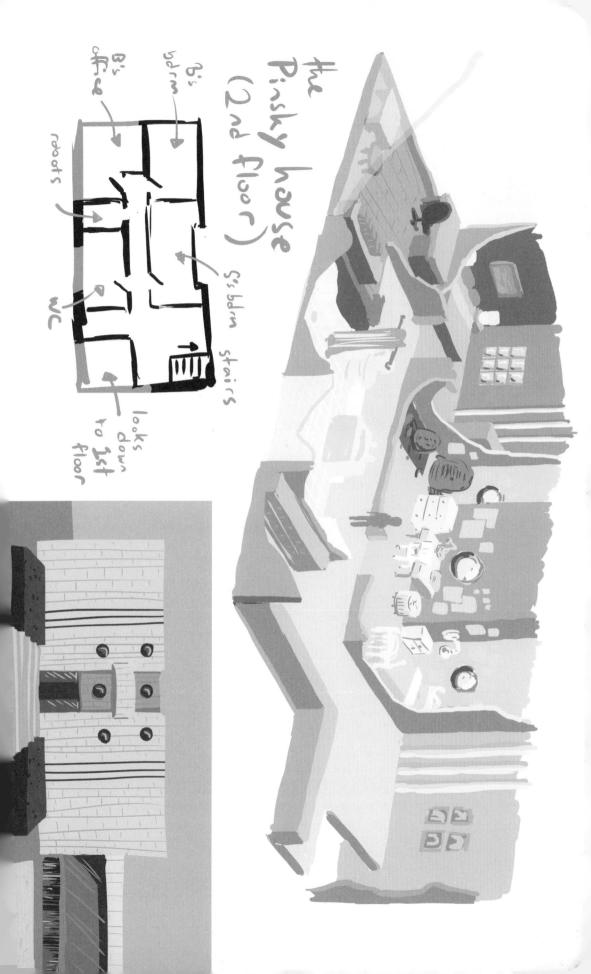

the
Pinsky house
(2nd floor)

B's office

B's bdrm

robots

WC

S's bdrm   stairs

looks down to 1st floor

Blue Delliquanti lives in an old house
in Minneapolis, Minnesota.
She enjoys riding trains, eating unusual
foods, and going to her local library.
You can continue reading *O Human Star*
at **ohumanstar.com** and view
the rest of her comics and art at
bluedelliquanti.com